"I'm not very good at secrets."

Paxton advanced on Ivy carefully, step by step from across the room. Each move made her heart pound.

How could a simple walk be sexy enough for her body to react?

"Are you lying?" he asked, drawing out each word.

Nerves caused her throat to close up, refusing to let out the words. She shook her head. She couldn't let Paxton find out about her family. Not yet.

"I think you are." His voice deepened, taking on a sexy, teasing tone that she'd thought she'd never hear again. "What do I need to do to get to the truth?"

He couldn't ever know the truth.

Danger seemed to shimmer between them. Ivy knew she shouldn't mess with the undercurrents she felt, but this game wasn't in her hands anymore.

Paxton kept moving forward, holding her gaze, until he came close enough to bury his hands in her hair.

His husky voice sent shivers over her body as he asked, "Are you sure there's nothing you want to tell me?"

* * *

Son of Scandal is part of the
Savannah Sisters series from Dani Wade.

Dear Reader,

My heroine in *Son of Scandal*, Ivy Harden, ends up with a world of heartache after a one-night stand with her boss, Paxton McLemore. Her dreams of falling in love with him and having a family are quickly dashed the morning after.

Ivy has some pretty tough choices to make in this book, but I'm proud of her for never completely letting go of her dream—even when it doesn't turn out quite the way she expected. I hope you enjoy the final installment of my Savannah Sisters trilogy!

I love to hear from my readers! You can email me at readdaniwade@gmail.com or follow me on Facebook. As always, news about my releases is easiest to find through my author newsletter, which you can sign up for from my website at www.daniwade.com.

Enjoy!

Dani

DANI WADE

———

SON OF SCANDAL

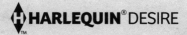
HARLEQUIN® DESIRE

Recycling programs
for this product may
not exist in your area.

ISBN-13: 978-1-335-60354-8

Son of Scandal

Copyright © 2019 by Katherine Worsham

For questions and comments about the quality of this book, please contact us at CustomerService@Harlequin.com.

Printed in U.S.A.

Dani Wade astonished her local librarians as a teenager when she carried home ten books every week—and actually read them all. Now she writes her own characters, who clamor for attention in the midst of the chaos that is her life. Residing in the Southern United States with a husband, two kids, two dogs and one grumpy cat, she stays busy until she can closet herself away with her characters once more.

Books by Dani Wade

Harlequin Desire

His by Design
Reining in the Billionaire
Unbridled Billionaire
A Family for the Billionaire

Milltown Millionaires

A Bride's Tangled Vows
The Blackstone Heir
The Renegade Returns
Expecting His Secret Heir

Savannah Sisters

Taming the Billionaire
Son of Scandal

Visit her Author Profile page at Harlequin.com, or daniwade.com, for more titles.

This book is dedicated to everyone
who helped me through one of the hardest times
in my life, also known as January 2018.
My sister, Ella (as always!). My mother.
My husband and children. My coworkers.
The Playfriends. My editor.
And all the readers and author friends
who reached out to me on Facebook to offer
encouragement and prayers.

This book would never have been
finished without you!

One

"Dance with me?"

Ivy looked at the outstretched hand, surprised and nonplussed at the same time. Her own fingers clenched over the itch in her palm. The itch that told her to reach out, to take what she coveted.

After a year and a half of carefully keeping Paxton McLemore at arm's length, did she dare step in close for a waltz?

They were at a masquerade ball, after all. The most glamorous charity event of the year, planned by her sister Jasmine Harden, Savannah's most noted event planner. Dancing with Paxton would be a natural action. One that wouldn't be judged by those around them, even though he was her employer. But she would know. Could she successfully hide how she felt when she was that close?

Though he wore a traditional black mask, she'd recognize his brilliant amber eyes anywhere—not just because of the intense color, but also the ever-present flash of intelligence and intuition she observed every day as his executive assistant.

It was just a dance... Why did she hesitate?

Suddenly he wiggled the fingers of the hand she had left dangling by her indecision. She smiled; the silly gesture was a charming reminder of the light-hearted moments they shared every day at work.

Ivy finally reached her hand out to his.

"You know, there's been a change in my office," Paxton said as his warm fingers curled around hers. "This new assistant came to work for me, and she makes me smile every day."

A glow warmed Ivy's core as he lifted her hand to graze her knuckles with his sculpted lips. She glanced down at their clasped hands as Paxton led her toward the dance floor in Keller House's renovated ballroom.

Though she should be focused on doing her part to make sure the incredible masquerade ball her sister had orchestrated ran smoothly, Ivy let thoughts of caterers and fund-raisers and responsibility fall away. But with a single touch, the struggle to breathe became real. It took her a moment to realize the truth— Paxton had never touched her before this.

Oh, she went out of her way to make him smile at the office, to soften the strain of his intense focus on work. Though her crush had intensified since she'd been working for him, she'd kept her actions and words strictly professional.

No touching. Until tonight.

Before she could register what was happening, they'd moved onto the dance floor and Paxton had turned to face her. He opened his arms, inviting her in. Ivy blinked—once, twice.

This is dangerous.

She chose to ignore her mind's warnings. Ivy stepped forward, and they took the waltz position, but didn't move. Instead Paxton's eyes widened at the initial contact, as if he, too, could feel the electric shock as they embraced.

Then his eyelids lowered to half-mast, taking on a slumberous, sexy look. A look she'd only seen in her fantasies.

Her heartbeat sped up, thrumming at the base of her throat. He took the first step, leading her in a modern-day version of the traditional dance.

Even though the warning bells she'd been silencing for a year were back full force, Ivy let his arms close around her, pull her closer. As they danced under the crystal chandeliers, amid dozens of other couples in the impeccably restored ballroom, the moment felt surreal. Out of time. His black tux was classic. The striking contrast between it and her emerald-green ball gown caught her eye as they glided past the wall of ornately framed mirrors.

The decadent illusion was dangerous—just like him.

She'd tried hard since her parents died to be practical, independent. But a small, hidden part of her still clung to the fantasy of fairy tales and Prince Charming.

Tonight, that part of her refused to be denied.

So she let him lead her, turn her, bend her to his touch. The touch that she'd fantasized about for the last year and a half she'd worked for him. During their daily routine, she'd resisted the pull of attraction, attempted to distract herself with clients and travel arrangements and meeting preparations. She'd thrown herself into the busy schedule of the head of the manufacturing division of his family's shipping conglomerate. But at the most unexpected of moments, she'd find herself immersed in far more intimate thoughts than she should have about her boss.

Tonight, he was that dream come to life. His touch and the intensity of his gaze made her feel beautiful, wanted. Her body tingled whenever he pressed close. This far surpassed her simple fantasies. The feelings were intense. Impossible to ignore.

They moved through the sea of people as if alone. The way her heart raced and her skin tingled with every brush of his hand was pure magic.

Every time logic attempted to assert itself, the intensity of his stare pushed it back. She wanted nothing more than to be his entire focus and let reality melt away.

He drew her closer, cocooning her in his arms. His gaze turned hungrier. His body grew harder.

Somewhere in the intensity, Ivy's resistance evaporated and she knew she'd go wherever he led her.

Even when the song was over and she had left him to do her hostessing rounds for her sister, she caught glimpses of him nearby. No matter how close or how far away, she could sense exactly where he was in the crowd. And it wasn't long before they found each other again in the muffled quiet of the front foyer.

Ivy held her breath, uncertainty washing over her. "Paxton…"

"I know," he said, reaching out to rub a finger over the velvet ribbon that held her mask in place. "I didn't expect this either. But I can't deny that I want you…very much."

He leaned into her, his mint-scented breath making her mouth water.

"We shouldn't…" she whispered, though her eyelids were already fluttering closed.

"I know…" He groaned.

Then his mouth covered hers and all protests were lost.

His kiss was just this side of demanding. Her body melted in acquiescence. He pressed closer, as if to absorb her surrender and claim his victory.

She knew how the night would end, and couldn't find an ounce of hesitation in her mind or body. Not even when he had paused, giving logic an opening to fracture the fantasy.

"I know I shouldn't ask you, that I have no right," Paxton said, the intensity of his stare making her shiver. "But, Ivy, will you go home with me?"

In that moment fantasy ruled. Though she'd denied it for over a year, Ivy had never wanted anything more than she wanted to spend tonight in Paxton's arms. "Yes. Yes, I will."

The happiness and excitement Ivy felt left her in a very surreal place, as if she couldn't quite grasp the reality of the decision she'd made.

Still she forced herself to be practical for one moment and made a quick call to her sister Jasmine. Hunting her down in the throngs of people would take too long. As she waited for Paxton to get the car brought around, Ivy heard the hesitation and concern in her sister's voice. Her tone escalated to alarm as Ivy told her where she was going but Ivy couldn't bring herself to care.

She'd spent the past year ignoring her family's secret connection to Paxton's. She justified taking the position with him by telling herself that he never had to know who she really was. Becoming his assistant had been a dream job for someone her age. With her drive to stand on her own two feet, there was no way she could have passed up such an incredible opportunity to advance. Or the temptation it had presented. Yes, it was a foolish hope. But maybe, just maybe, this was the right thing.

She glanced at the teardrop emerald on her right ring finger, swearing it actually twinkled in the subdued lighting on the front stone steps, where she waited. The piece of jewelry handed down to her and her sisters through generations of their family, who believed its magic would guide them to find their true love.

The professional Ivy wanted to scoff at the notion

that the ring had anything to do with what was happening tonight. But the princess wannabe she hid deep down inside regarded the ring with a smile before she glanced up to see Paxton step out of the back of the company limo.

"Come with me?" he asked, reaching his hand out to her.

She knew what was happening. Knew he was giving her a way out at the same time that he made his preference known. He was a gentleman, through and through. Tonight, she wanted him to be hers.

He quickly handed her into the dim interior, which got even darker as he closed the door behind him. The driver pulled away from the curb right away. Paxton wasn't wasting time on niceties. His urgency mirrored hers—much to her relief.

Paxton immediately distracted her from thoughts of rings, sisters and the fact that he was her boss. In the private world of the back seat, he embraced her without hesitation. Their decision was made.

He cupped her head in his large, warm hands, holding her steady for his kiss. In the tight space, every breath, every gasp, every moan was amplified. Then his hands traveled downward, heating up her neck, collarbone and the tops of her breasts. The air stuttered in her lungs as she ached for him to slip his hand beneath the edge of her dress. Instead his mouth followed the trail, creating a heated path of sizzling nerves. She arched into the pull of his lips and tongue and teeth against her skin.

Then he was slipping away from her, pulling back

from the grip of her fingers around his upper arms. But the disappointment was quickly replaced by a thrill of both fear and need as he insinuated his big body between the V-shape of her thighs.

The thickly layered skirt of her ball gown proved no match for Paxton. She felt his long fingers close around her ankles in a firm grip, tight enough to let her know he was there without leaving a mark. Her thighs clenched as everything inside her tightened. She needed to surrender to that touch, to let him do with her what he chose.

His fingers traced down over her four-inch heels, a rumbling groan rolling out of his chest. A half smile escaped her, one he might see in the occasional street-lights they passed. They were nearing the city now.

Slowly his palms traced upward, beneath the layers of material. Cupping her calves. Rubbing her knees. Massaging her thighs. Ivy panted as she grew wet with need. Would he touch her there? Or would he leave her to wait?

His fingertips found the line of her garters. "Heaven help me, Ivy." Without warning, he bunched up the heavy skirt and disappeared beneath it. His hands curled around her knees and pulled her forward. She felt open and vulnerable. She swallowed hard, wishing now for just a hint of the logic that had made a brief appearance earlier.

But it was nowhere to be seen.

His mouth met the tender skin right above the top of her thigh-high stockings, sucking hard as if he could swallow her into him. Her muscles tightened as

if to push him away, but the move was merely instinc-
tual. Truthfully, she wanted him to taste her there…
wanted him to taste her more. His tongue flicked
firmly along the upper lace edge, then along the garter, until he buried his face in the crook between her
thigh and hip. She felt the breath he drew with every
nerve ending in her body.

Abruptly the car halted, the brakes applied with a
little more force than necessary.

But it was enough to bring Paxton to his senses.
Thank goodness, because any mindfulness she had
was long gone. Paxton made quick and careful work
of returning her skirt to its original modest position.
Then he opened the door and stepped outside. She
heard him speaking with the driver, but when he
reached in to help her out, the man was back behind
the wheel. The car was speeding down the drive before Paxton had her halfway up his front walk.

Now they were alone together. No audience. Just
the night and the two of them. The perfect ingredi-
ents for her own incredible fairy tale.

Paxton woke to incredible warmth.

The sun shining through the half-closed curtains
heated the cool room. The tangle of his legs with the
woman asleep beside him heated his skin. His body
was alive with urgent need.

Then his brain kicked into gear.

Where it had been last night, he wasn't sure. His
body tightened as images rose from his memory. The
full impact of what they'd done hit him in a rush.

His assistant. He'd spent the night with his assistant.

An incredible night...

He breathed deeply, attempting to mitigate the odd mix of desire and panic. To slow his racing heartbeat, cool his body's ardor. Because they couldn't do this again.

He'd been such a fool.

Paxton glanced over at Ivy. She faced away from him, but the smooth curve of her shoulder and waterfall of tangled blond hair drew him. Her beauty made him reach out to touch, but he clenched his hand into a fist instead to stop himself.

Last night he'd been blindsided by the need to bury his hands in that silky blond hair. He licked his lips as he remembered the taste of her skin last night, of her full lips, plump breasts and soft thighs. And that garter!

A flash of fever heated his bare skin.

But as he watched the sun flirt with her as she slept, the panic lurking in the background simply wouldn't go away. What had he been thinking?

Well, he hadn't been.

He urgently needed coffee; it would be a welcome distraction. He eased from the bed, careful not to rouse Ivy, reminding himself that she must be exhausted. She'd spent the last week working her full-time job with him, then helping her sister out with the charity ball. Then she'd spent all day Saturday preparing for the event, and Saturday night splitting the hostessing duties.

She had every right to be tired…and to sleep in.

Leaving her asleep had nothing to do with not wanting to face her…not wanting to tell her this could absolutely not go any further than it already had.

As he headed to the kitchen, he heard the faint noise of his phone vibrating against the foyer table. Instinctively he made a detour for it. One glance at the display told him his executive VP was on the other end of the line—and weekend calls were definitely not his thing. Paxton's senses geared up for whatever emergency was coming his way.

"What's up, Mike?"

"Where the heck have you been? I've been calling since 5:00 a.m."

Paxton clenched his jaw. "I'm here now," he said.

"We've got a problem," Mike said, ignoring his tight tone. "Remember how we took a chance on not replacing the old super engine?"

Paxton groaned. His manufacturing plant in Virginia had been a buyout that they were in the process of refurbishing and upgrading. He'd had a tough time convincing his grandmother, who was still chairwoman of the board, that it was a worthwhile endeavor. This could be a major setback.

Mike went on. "Yep. It blew during the night. I'm gonna need some help out here."

Which meant catching the first flight out to Virginia ASAP. Paxton would need to be on site to formulate his plan for the repairs or replacement, while still keeping the plant functioning. He signed off, then sighed. Not a good morning for this. The only

thing he wanted was coffee, and the chance to figure out what he needed to say to the woman whom
he'd had the most inappropriate skin-to-skin contact
with ever in his life.

Well, maybe not *the* most…but he didn't want to
think about the past mistake that made him believe
the present situation could end in doom, too.

Knowing he needed to get a move on, Paxton
headed upstairs to the master suite to shower and
then pack his bag. He felt a moment of relief when
he remembered how he'd rushed Ivy into one of the
downstairs bedrooms last night because he couldn't
wait to get her undressed, and because that was simply his MO with women.

At least he wouldn't be haunted by memories of
the passion they'd shared every night when he would
lie down in his own bed.

He quickly finished dressing, then threw some
clothes into a duffel bag. A few days at the plant in
Virginia, then he and Ivy could have a nice long talk
about what had happened between them last night.
And what should happen between them now. Paxton
had his future mapped out to a *T*. And his family was
fully behind him. Marrying his assistant was not in
his life plan.

Paxton hoped Ivy was on the same wavelength.

On his way out, he paused in the shadowy doorway of the downstairs bedroom. Ivy still slept, oblivious to his dilemma. He felt the urge to crawl back
into that sun-kissed space beside her. He even took a
single step forward.

But duty called.

His phone started vibrating in his pocket, warning him time was of the essence. In a quick scrawl, he wrote a note, letting Ivy know that he'd had to run, but she could call the car to take her home. He'd be back soon…and they would talk then.

Still he carried the memories of her sun-warmed skin and everything they'd done to each other in the dark of night as he rode to the airport, paced the VIP Lounge and then boarded the first standby flight he could get for Virginia. He thought a few times about texting her…but it just seemed like such an impersonal, lousy thing to do.

Maybe after a few days away, they could both gain some perspective on what they wanted, how they could return to their steady, professional relationship. Right? He rubbed his palm over his face. Hell, what if this blew up in his face big time?

He remembered the sun glinting off her loose mane of golden hair this morning. Why had she been hiding it in a severe ponytail all this time? Oh, he knew. His buttoned-up executive admin was the utmost professional. Hair always pulled back. Business suits, but only with skirts. He'd always been grateful that she didn't cover up the smooth curve of her calves with dress pants. Instead she accentuated it by wearing smart, sexy heels.

He gulped the last of his hot, black coffee as the plane began to descend.

Of course, he'd been careful to only look when she was walking away from him. Still she'd caught him looking a time or two. Just like he'd found her doing the same. And even though there'd been definite sparks in the air every time they'd locked gazes in the office, neither of them had been willing to break the status quo. Until last night.

They'd been playing with fire, not realizing just when it would blow up.

Paxton forced himself to pick up his bag from the luggage carousel, and then headed outside to flag down a taxi. Mike had his hands full right now, so Paxton had told him not to worry about sending a car. As he settled into the back seat, he read the half dozen text messages waiting for him from Mike. Each one was worse than the next. Paxton may have gotten his start in industry through his family name and his grandmother's owning the umbrella conglomerate, but his diverse interests, determination and leadership skills had earned him the success he enjoyed today as the CEO of an international shipping parts manufacturer...with his eye on running the entire conglomerate one day.

So why was his mind on the woman who was still asleep in his house, instead of the major issues awaiting him at the factory?

Two

Two months later...

"**P**axton. You there, big brother?"

Paxton snapped to attention to find Sierra frowning at him. She had every right. He'd stepped in to take her to the obstetrician today, toddler in tow, while her husband was out of town. He should be present in mind and body, but thoughts of Ivy and all that had happened since his return home yesterday kept distracting him.

Marshalling his powers of concentration, he stepped out of the car and circled around to free his niece from her car seat in the back.

Just when he'd thought he and Ivy would be okay, that their professional life would move forward just as he'd wanted it to, she'd sent him her resignation via email. It had arrived while he'd been on the plane home, so it had been the first thing to catch his eye when he'd landed.

"So, what kept you away so long?" his sister asked.

"I was only supposed to be gone a few days. A week, tops." The reality had been a nightmare. "One mechanical problem led to another, then another. At one point we actually had to shut down production for over twenty-four hours."

"I bet Grandmother was thrilled," Sierra said with a conspiratorial smile.

Oh, she'd been none too happy to hear it, reminding him she wasn't cutting him any slack just because he was her grandson. He still had to justify every expense and setback.

At least it had distracted him from thoughts of Ivy. And as the days rolled into weeks, neither of them had mentioned their night together, even though they spoke on the phone almost every day and emailed even more than that. Their conversations had been strictly business, and Paxton had been perfectly happy with that.

He'd thought Ivy had been, too.

By the time he'd made it back to his house and dropped his luggage in the master suite, Paxton had convinced himself her resignation was for the best. Obviously she hadn't wanted to face him in person. He could understand that. Their night together had been a bigger mistake on his part. As her boss, he bore the weight of responsibility and should be grateful she hadn't accused him of sexual harassment, despite their intimacy being mutual. He should probably reach out with a severance package to keep her from bearing any burdens while she looked for another job. Would she accept? Or was she angry that he'd stuck strictly to business all this time?

Still he couldn't stop thinking about her. A woman he should be grateful was gone.

He needed his head examined.

"You must be living on another planet today. Did you leave your brain in Virginia?" his sister demanded, her normally calm demeanor showing strain as she pulled her daughter from his arms.

Paxton took a deep breath, trying to regain his equilibrium. "I just have a lot on my mind."

Sierra led the way across the parking lot, toward the office building. "Just so long as it's work and not a woman. Grandmother would have a fit if you didn't keep your priorities straight."

The bitterness in her voice immediately caught Paxton's attention. He stared at her in surprise.

His family members were founders and high-ranking business leaders of Savannah society. They'd been taught to marry well, aim high and value family over all else. He'd grown up looking forward to starting one of his own, and he'd been groomed to marry the woman who would best enhance his professional and personal profile. Just like his sisters, who'd chosen their husbands from elite Savannah families.

That was the plan—one that didn't include Ivy. Yet he'd wanted her since he'd first laid eyes on her.

And nothing had prepared him for the ecstasy of actually having her.

Except, according to the map he'd laid out for his life, he couldn't keep her. He'd stepped out of his comfort zone in the name of romance and knew it was a mistake.

But that wasn't something you said to a woman over the phone.

"What?" Sierra demanded.

Her sharp tone had him looking closer. Paxton couldn't miss the strain in his sister's expression. Some people might attribute it to the fatigue of her being in the second trimester of pregnancy while taking care of his very active niece, but Paxton knew better. The tight muscles around her eyes and tart tone weren't normal for her.

He slowed her down with a hand on her arm, easing her over to one side of the hallway outside of the doctor's office. His niece had gotten sleepy, laying her heavy head on her mom's shoulder.

"Are you okay?" he asked in a quiet tone, pulling himself forcibly back to the here and now. "What's up?"

As if realizing just how much she'd revealed, Sierra glanced away. But Paxton didn't miss the rapid blinking of her eyes against the sudden tears. "Nothing. It's probably just the hormones."

While that could definitely play a part, his big-brother instincts told him something more was going on. "Is everything okay?" He thought back over her words. "Is there a problem between you and Jason?"

"I wouldn't know," she sniffed, then reached up to

stroke her sleepy daughter's hair. "He's always at work. Though I guess that's what I married him for...right?"

She turned back to him after only a few steps. "Take it from me, Paxton," she said in a low tone. "Just because the whole business-before-pleasure thing worked for our parents and grandparents doesn't mean it's the wonderful life they told us it would be. Marrying for money is just as complicated as marrying for love."

Then she quickly changed the subject. "Let's check in," she said, almost too nonchalantly. He knew she was trying to hide from him as she reached for the door.

He'd never known her to keep secrets, but her stoic facade worried him.

Following Sierra and his niece into the doctor's waiting room, Paxton felt that familiar surge of protectiveness that he often got by just hanging out with his siblings. They'd always been close. Add in the gaggle of girl children his sisters had given birth to, and Paxton found himself to be a hands-on uncle. His grandmother often prophesied that Paxton would be the first to give the family a male heir, something he definitely looked forward to. But until then he would protect and love the women in his life as much as possible.

If he only knew what Sierra needed protecting from...

"Here," he said, reaching out for his niece, "let me take her while you sign in."

He snuggled the droopy toddler in his arms and stood behind his sister as the receptionist opened the window that separated her from the waiting room. Small talk floated around him as Sierra signed the check-in list; he wasn't really paying attention. He glanced over the women's heads, farther into the little box the receptionist occupied. Behind her, at the exit window, a woman in scrubs was speaking to a patient who was checking out. At first Paxton couldn't see her. Then she turned toward him.

Ivy.

Without a thought, Paxton leaned closer to the opening. He knew he shouldn't eavesdrop, but it was if his hearing was tuned in specifically to her voice. Luckily for him, his hearing was excellent.

"Here are your vitamins," the woman in scrubs said.

Ivy had a nervous expression as she glanced down at the box on the checkout counter. Paxton's gaze followed. He swallowed hard. The words *prenatal vitamins* seemed to jump out at him.

The woman continued, oblivious to the audience behind her. "And this is a prescription for nausea medicine. Take it when you need it, which will hopefully only be for another month or so. You and the baby need good nutrition right now, so we don't want you too sick to eat. Got it?"

Ivy nodded, swallowing hard enough for Paxton to see her throat working. Nausea? Prenatal vitamins? Baby? The words floated through the fog clouding his brain. He blinked, trying to process. He knew what the words meant, but he couldn't get the significance to register.

Just then, Ivy looked across the tiny room and spotted him. Her eyes went wide. Her lips parted, but no words came out. He didn't need any. Panic spread across her features like a wave, putting the final piece in the puzzle.

A baby. They'd made a baby?

No sooner had he blinked than she was gone. He couldn't see which way she went through the receptionist's window.

"Paxton, what is wrong with you today?" his sister complained.

He glanced down to realize the way he was leaning had her blocked in against the check-in counter. "Sorry," he mumbled. "Here."

He handed his niece over to her mother, then murmured, "I'll be right back."

Remembering the office layout from the few times he'd been there before, Paxton knew the exit let out on the other side of the clinic, but then patients had to come back up the front hallway to get to the parking lot. He rushed back out the way they'd come in, hoping to intercept Ivy. Not that he knew what he'd say. His only thought was to find her. Now.

The hallway was empty. He backtracked down the hall to the adjoining one, but still didn't see her. Maybe she'd already gotten outside? But he couldn't find her in the parking lot either. He cursed himself as he realized he wasn't even sure what kind of car she drove. After a good five minutes—and one missed call and exasperated text from his sister—Paxton returned to the doctor's waiting room.

But Ivy's panicked features remained foremost in his mind.

"Paxton McLemore saw me at the obstetrician's office."

The heart-pounding panic as Ivy spoke the words

to her sisters was almost overwhelming. She forced herself to breathe in and out slowly. This intense upset couldn't be good for the child she carried. Even if it was justified. She'd spent a month second-guessing herself, only to have all her plans smashed with one doctor's visit.

"What happened?" Jasmine asked, her voice hushed with expectation. Jasmine was the epitome of the older sister, fulfilling her role with wisdom and the same matter-of-fact tone she used on unruly clients in her event planning business.

"I looked up from the counter, and there he stood. Watching me." Ivy swallowed. So tall. With a baby sleeping in his arms, he'd almost seemed like her fantasies come to life. Only it wasn't their child. And the realization that she was truly seeing Paxton in that moment had been more like a nightmare.

One that mocked the dreams of happily-ever-after she'd been rudely woken from that fateful morning, two months ago.

"He recognized you, I hope?" Auntie asked, her frown deepening the wrinkles on her beloved face.

Oh, he had. "Yes. There was recognition in his eyes. Then shock." Her finger traced the interlocking pattern of the tiger wood on the dining room table.

Ivy had watched Paxton's gaze drop to the box on the counter with the paralyzing realization of what was to come…and knowing she could do nothing to stop it. Luckily the nurse had wrapped things up quickly.

She imagined her disappearing act would not go

over well with Paxton once he got over the shock. "I panicked. I didn't know what to do, what to say." She looked around, shame burning her cheeks. "So I just grabbed my stuff and ran."

A little giggle sounded to her left. Ivy cast a quick glance at Willow. "What's so funny?" she demanded.

Willow pressed her lips together, but it didn't help since her amusement was evident to everyone. Their middle sister had always marched to her own drum. "Well, all I can imagine is you running down the hall, pushing people out of the way, like one of those victims in a thriller movie. In heels, no less." She giggled again. "Not your normal modus operandi."

Auntie started to chuckle, then Jasmine. In less than sixty seconds, they were all giggling until the tears started. Even Ivy. She drew in a deep breath. Man, that felt good. No one could make her laugh when she needed it like her sisters.

"Maybe he won't care?" Willow asked, sober once more. How could she sound skeptical and hopeful at the same time?

Ivy forced herself to wipe away the last of her tears. She'd been reliving that awful moment when she'd looked up to see Paxton staring at her from across the little office for hours now. She'd finally realized his sister had been with him. At least his being there made some sort of sense now.

Even though it was still disastrous.

Auntie cut into her thoughts, offering the same steady wisdom she'd handed out to the girls since she'd taken them in as orphaned teenagers. "Oh, he will care. The question is, what will he do about it? Men like him never quit."

As Ivy felt her stomach tighten in protest, Jasmine admonished, "Auntie, that's not helping."

"Doesn't make it less true," Auntie insisted.

How could she have gotten herself into this mess? With Paxton McLemore, of all people? "Why did I wear that ring?" She moaned, letting her head drop into her hands. "Why did I think it would bring anything but bad luck?"

"Because it produced miracles for Jasmine and me?" Willow asked.

This was really not a good moment for both of her sisters to remind Ivy that they'd found their happily-ever-afters while wearing the ring. She hadn't been so lucky.

Ivy glared at Willow. "Too bad I didn't get the same treatment."

But she couldn't truly blame the ring. She'd let fantasies overtake her since the first day she'd started working for Paxton McLemore, at the expense of her true mission. Keep her head down, work hard and get ahead—all without him discovering who she really was. Playing with fire had gotten her burned. Now her family could be in as much trouble as she was... if Paxton pursued her too closely and discovered who they really were.

"He hasn't called, even though he has your personal cell number," Jasmine said, obviously trying to change the subject. "Even though it's only been a few hours, that's a good sign, right?"

"I don't know," Ivy said and then moaned.

"Will he realize the baby is his?" Auntie asked.

"There's no way Paxton McLemore won't put two and two together." They'd used a condom, but mistakes happen.

Ivy worried the inside of her bottom lip with her teeth. She didn't doubt Paxton would contact her at some point. He might not care anything about her—he'd made that clear over the last two months. But a baby... Paxton was a family man through and through. She doubted he would ignore her pregnancy, no matter how much of an inconvenience it was to him. "I have no idea what to say to him."

A banging on the front door startled them all. "Geesh," Willow exclaimed. "Take it easy."

She headed down the hallway. Jasmine's hand covered Ivy's, warming her chilled skin. "Everything's gonna be okay," she murmured.

Why didn't Ivy feel the same way?

They heard Willow open the door and say something, followed by a deep, smooth male voice.

"Where is she?"

Ivy's eyes widened, her gaze locking with Jasmine's. There was no mistaking Paxton's voice or the forceful tone that she'd heard time and again in business meetings. The panic from earlier returned full force, drumming in her chest. She and Jasmine scrambled from their seats.

Together, they peeked around the door frame of the dining room, straight down the hall. Paxton stood in the front doorway with an angry expression on his face. In that moment he glanced over Willow's shoulder and saw Ivy.

He didn't bother asking for permission. Instead he shouldered past Ivy's sister and stomped down the hallway, causing the wooden floors to creak in protest.

"Paxton," Ivy exclaimed. "What are you doing here?"

"Hunting down what's mine."

A small part of her was thrilled at his words, but the anger in his expression told her in no uncertain terms that he wasn't here for her. At least, not the way she wanted.

"Get out!" The words escaped her mouth just as Auntie murmured, "I told you so."

A hint of amusement passed over Paxton's face before he turned grim again. "If I'm understanding this situation correctly, you turned in your resignation and walked away, knowing you were pregnant with my child?"

A chorus of feminine "oh dears" filled the air and guilt struck Ivy hard. Yes, that's exactly what she'd done. But his blunt recitation of the facts didn't truly represent the whole picture: her loneliness and fear and anger over the past two months.

"Ivy," Paxton said, his timbre low and menacing. He stopped directly in front of her, looming just enough to inspire a touch of fear. "It seems we have a problem."

Three

"Do I get any kind of explanation?"

"Do you deserve one?" Under other circumstances, Ivy had plenty of reserves to pull from to keep herself diplomatic. But Paxton's appearance here had her off guard and on edge.

She needed her sisters. A glance toward the doorway from the kitchen showed that it was empty. Ivy licked her dry lips. When Paxton had asked to speak with her alone, they'd reluctantly left for the front parlor. Not that they wouldn't come running if she yelled, but still…she couldn't stop herself from wrapping her arms around her middle.

Facing him alone made her stomach hurt even more than when she'd just been worrying over him showing up.

"How'd you find me?" she asked.

"Human resources was nice enough to help with an address."

She licked her lips again. "Why?"

"Seriously?"

Ivy was genuinely surprised as Paxton's eyes widened and his tone deepened with more anger. She wasn't sure why. Paxton was passionate about kids. But the knowledge that he was here for that reason alone made her own anger surge.

"I could have been at the doctor's office for any number of reasons..." she insisted.

"Like getting a prescription of prenatal vitamins?"

"That was none of your business, Paxton."

"Don't even go there..." he growled.

He leaned closer, his height giving him the advantage. His intention might not be intimidation, but it sure felt that way. Even in her heels, she'd never come close to his height. In her current flip-flops, she didn't stand a chance. But at least she was still on her feet. Sitting down felt like giving him too much of an advantage, so she continued to stand, even though her body swayed under the continuous onslaught of pregnancy hormones, nausea and exhaustion.

Paxton wasn't through throwing his weight around. "If you simply wanted to walk away from your job, that's your prerogative. But with my child? No way."

The possessiveness in his words sent a scary thrill through her. "*My* child," she insisted.

"Your words earlier already told me it's mine, too."

He smirked. "You can't deny it. I was listening at the window. I heard it all."

How would it feel to be able to wipe that smirk off his face?

If she'd known he was listening, she'd have been careful not to give so much away. *Eavesdropper.* But then, Paxton was used to having his way in life. She'd seen it time and again when she worked for him. It would be best to set some boundaries up front. "A little beneath you, isn't it?"

"I could say the same. Sneaking around. Running away. You could have just told me."

In that moment it felt like Ivy's blood turned to jet fuel and someone set a match to it. Heated fury instantly engulfed her. She stomped forward. "At what point? You made it clear you weren't interested in hearing anything personal. And you certainly didn't seem to be interested in any consequences before today."

He shook his head. "This is a child we're talking about here."

Obviously that's all that mattered. "I see. The only consequences of note are the ones that affect you."

He stalked away, steps heavy on the kitchen's tile floor, and raked his hands through his blond hair in a familiar gesture she'd seen so many times in his office. Frustration. Anger. It took a lot to push Paxton that far. When those emotions overtook him in public, he simply went cold in his expression, movements and words.

Not in private. That was the part she already

missed—all the emotions she'd been privy to that Paxton rarely showed anyone outside his family.

Unfortunately, now the emotions were directed at her. And not the fiercely tender ones she remembered from their one night together.

After several rounds of pacing, he settled in a chair at the table, then gestured for her to do the same. The stubborn part of her that wouldn't rest today wanted to insist he wasn't her boss anymore. She'd sit when she was good and ready. But the invitation rather than demand in his simple motion made her stubbornness seem petty.

Damn him.

She sat across from him, uncomfortably reminded of the many business negotiations she'd seen him participate in, sitting just this way. Facing his opponent dead-on. He didn't let them know they were opponents. Oh no. He greeted them with a charming smile and handshake. Otherwise he'd be giving too much away.

She unconsciously braced herself as he leaned her way.

"Why?" he asked, his voice soft but with an undercurrent of steel. "Were you ever going to tell me?"

She bit her lip, feeling heartless. But what could she say? She hadn't truly decided what she was going to do. Right now, every day was about survival: submitting résumés for another job, getting enough food in her so she didn't pass out, but not so much that she threw up.

Not an easy balancing act.

Finally she sighed, then attempted to put her thoughts into words. "Eventually…" She swallowed, studying the intricate pattern of light and dark wood pieces fitted together to create the handmade table where so many big family discussions had taken place in her life. "Once I had things figured out and stable, I would have let you know."

"And what needs to be figured out?" His voice had gone low again, this time with warning.

Surprised, she glanced over at him. She'd known that Paxton was unusually devoted to his family and doted on all of his nieces. Every bit of that protective instinct was alive and well in his expression right now. But not for her…never for her. "Obviously a new job," she said, hurt clipping her words.

"Obviously?"

"Yes, Paxton." Her exasperation left her breathy. "Regardless of what happens between us or with this pregnancy, working together after this would not be pleasant…or professional."

"Why not? Can't you separate your emotions from your job?"

Not that much. "Don't be ridiculous, Paxton."

"What happened between us—"

"Was a mistake."

He froze for a split second, as if he couldn't believe her words. "Says who?"

"You—" she erupted, slapping her palm on the table with more force than she had intended. How dare he act like she was overreacting. "You did. With every phone call and email that contained plenty of instructions but a whole lot of nothing." She couldn't control the rise in volume. "You did this, Paxton."

"You never said anything."

"I slept with my boss!" She struggled for breath in the midst of her raging emotions. "When he leaves without waking you up and then never mentions it again, there could only be two explanations—he's either too drunk to remember what happened or refuses to acknowledge what happened. There's not a whole lot I can say to address either of those situations."

"I wasn't drunk," he said quietly.

"Which leaves only one alternative." Turning away, Ivy pressed her hand hard against her stomach. The chaotic emotions rushing through her did not help her morning sickness at all. Though why they called it that, she'd never know. Hers was more like morning, noon and night sickness.

"Are you okay?" Paxton asked, his voice sounding closer. Sure enough, a quick glance confirmed he was on his feet and halfway around the table already.

"No," she snapped. She breathed slow and deep, in through her nose, out through her mouth. So far the only things she'd found that helped when the nausea hit at its random times were to keep very still and stay calm. This situation wasn't conducive to either.

"Besides, there are other issues to consider."

"Like what?"

She realized he wasn't going to let her get away with not answering that question. But her brain was seriously on strike right now. Thinking things through wasn't her strong point. All she knew was that anything she said about her family could potentially do a lot of damage.

Not just for herself and any custody battles she found herself in, but also for Jasmine. Even though her sister had a fiancé with clout now, the news of the Harden sisters' true heritage could break her event-planning business if the McLemores decided to go after her.

"I can't… I can't talk about that right now. My stomach——" She hated to use illness to get herself out of this discussion, but at least this overwhelming sickness came in handy for something.

"Okay," he conceded.

But she had a feeling she wasn't getting off easy. Suddenly he stood before her with his legs braced and his arms crossed over his chest.

"But remember," he said, "I can't fix what I don't know."

"I'm not sure this can be fixed." Ivy gasped against a wave of nausea. "I just…I need time."

"We don't have an infinite amount of that left."

She glanced up to find him facing her, big body braced, arms crossed over his chest, causing his dress shirt to strain over smooth muscle. He opened his mouth. Then closed it. All while staring at her.

"What?" But she was almost afraid to ask. Paxton wasn't the type of guy to be at a loss for words.

"Did you do this on purpose?"

Wow. Ivy swayed. Or did she? Maybe it just felt that way with her mind reeling. She really had been delusional to think he might feel anything for her… hadn't she?

Her chest was too tight with hurt for her voice to

come out more than a whisper. "Is that really how you see me?"

His answer was too matter-of-fact for her liking. "No. But people can hide a lot."

Just like he had. He'd hidden a lot of suspicion behind caring, hadn't he? "There's nothing I can say to convince you that I didn't deliberately get pregnant, Paxton," she said with more resignation than conviction. "That's gonna be a problem, isn't it?"

"Probably."

She doesn't look so fierce in her sleep.

Paxton stared down at Ivy as she rested on the sofa in the Hardens' front parlor. Her tousled hair looked the same as it had on the morning that he'd left her in his bed, but her face was thinner now. A slight frown rested between her brows, as if she couldn't get comfortable, even in her sleep.

Uneasy with the softening of his emotional defenses, Paxton forced his gaze away from her to the surrounding room. He took in the antique furniture mixed with a few well-worn pieces and lots of soft feminine touches. The living space seemed well used and designed for comfort, while respecting the past.

"She's plumb tuckered out all the time," the older woman the sisters called Auntie said as she came up beside him.

Paxton glanced over at her, unease filtering through him. "Is this level of sickness dangerous? I don't remember either of my sisters having this problem."

Sierra rarely got sick at all. Janine had spent the

first three months throwing up every morning, then she was fine the rest of the day. But they were both very emotional—conversations could turn into mine-fields without warning.

"Oh, it isn't dangerous," Auntie said with a wave of her hand. "As long as we keep enough food in her, she and the baby will be fine. Not comfortable, by any stretch of the imagination. But safe."

Paxton suppressed a smile. "Good to know."

"It's all been rough on her—" Auntie went on, shift-ing slightly "—between the sickness, how this all came about and getting used to the idea of bringing a new life into the world. That's a lot for a girl to take in."

Paxton was well aware. "I bet."

"She'll be a good mama, though. You'll see."

Finally Paxton let his gaze return to the sleeping beauty. He knew Ivy to be capable, efficient, eter-nally prepared for any number of clients' demands. The night of the masquerade, he'd discovered just how passionate she could be. The last thing he'd wondered about her was what kind of mother she'd be.

Guess he better start considering the possibilities.

That's not why I'm here. Paxton shook his head slightly. He'd spent the night vacillating between sheer panic and endless questions. Not the joy that he'd felt each time his sisters had announced their pregnancies.

He'd realized immediately after leaving yesterday that he'd taken the wrong tack. Letting their emotions take control wouldn't get them anywhere. Especially not him. It was the first time he could remember his emotions overtaking his logic so completely. A scary place for him to be.

So he'd returned this afternoon for a bit of reconnaissance. His best option for moving forward and answering his own questions about this whole situation was information.

Information about Ivy outside of their professional exposure to each other. Information about her family and the environment the child would be born into. That way he could make decisions and plans based on what he thought was best.

This situation wasn't ideal. It was what it was. He just needed a plan of action.

He forced his gaze away. Focus on the plan. Not on the woman.

"Thank you for having me," he said, turning up the wattage on his smile as he glanced back at Auntie. Just as he had yesterday, he'd noticed her limp as she'd led him from the front door, into the parlor. She had the pinkish complexion of health, but also the slight droop of exhaustion in her expression. Even this early in the evening.

"Oh, these girls keep me busy," she said, "but it makes life happy, you know?"

"I do, indeed. My family is a big part of my life also."

And he was not looking forward to hearing their thoughts when they found out he'd gotten his assistant pregnant. Definitely not what they'd had in mind when they urged him to start a family. Of course, it wasn't what he'd had in mind, either. Family had been the last thing he'd been thinking about when he'd taken Ivy to bed that night.

"I love having a big family," Auntie was saying, "Even though they came to me later in life. Do you have a big family?"

Paxton smiled and chatted about his two sisters and all his nieces. He truly loved his family, even when they were driving him crazy. He'd always been close with his siblings and his parents and grandmother. As the only grandson, they had high expectations for him and his future family. Almost as high as he had for himself.

Having a baby with Ivy didn't fit into the plan. His stomach twisted as he imagined their disappointment. But regardless of whether this baby fit his stringent requirements for having children, the baby existed. Paxton was not the kind of man who could simply walk away.

It wasn't just about responsibilities, either. He'd spent a lot of time with his sisters and nieces. He didn't know where this was going, but those joyful thoughts of welcoming a child into the world and watching it grow were already taking hold.

Only a day, and he'd already been sucked in.

"Thank you for taking care of her," he said, in a sincere effort to show his appreciation, despite what Ivy would have thought if she'd heard it.

The older woman's smile was kind. "Ivy insists she's handling it, but it is wearing her down, I believe. She doesn't want anyone else to feel responsible, but that's what family does."

She leaned a little closer and lowered her voice. "I

even postponed a trip with her sister Jasmine because I just don't want her alone. And she needs her own bed right now, her own space. Not to be out at Willow's place, away from her comfort zone."

Paxton stared for just a moment, his brain kicking into overtime. Something started to take shape, but before he could analyze it, a soft voice drifted across the room.

"Somehow I knew you'd be back."

Paxton was unsettled by Ivy's resigned tone. Without thought, his chin went up and he said, "You shouldn't doubt it. We'll be a major part of each other's lives from here on out."

Inwardly he winced. Probably not the right approach at the moment. Unlike Ivy, Paxton knew he needed to keep his emotions out of this situation. He wasn't sure how he felt about Ivy. About her being the mother of his child. He'd attempted to put every spine-tingling moment of their night together out of his mind...and had succeeded until the moment he'd returned home. But he didn't want to think about it. Right now, he needed to focus on the child.

The one thing he refused to walk away from.

Not wanting to hover over her, Paxton crossed to the sofa, where she lay, and eased himself into the far corner. Ivy's eyes widened before she pushed herself into a more upright position and pulled her feet closer to her. But not before he caught sight of her delicate feet with their bright pink toenails.

Once more he struggled to push back the memories.

"I'll leave you youngins alone for a bit," Auntie

finally said, winking at Paxton. "I'm sure you have a lot to discuss."

Indeed they did.

Paxton turned back to Ivy, then winced at her cynical expression.

"Any particular reason you're trying to charm my aunt?"

Busted. "What are you talking about?"

"I've been watching you in action for a year and a half now. I've seen that same smile a hundred times. What are you trying to prove?"

That I'm not the bad guy here. "How are you feeling?" he asked, instead of answering her question.

She pushed the heavy fall of her hair back behind her ear. "Okay."

He could spot the lie from a mile away, even without her grimace.

"Medicine helping any?"

She glanced down at the floor as if she was uncomfortable with the attention. "It helps me not be sick, but doesn't take away the nausea altogether."

She'd lost weight, he noticed again. Her high cheekbones stood out more than they had, creating a hollow beneath. There were dark shadows under her eyes, too. She was indeed having a rough time of it.

"The doctor says only about a month more..." she said, her voice weak. "Then we should start to see some improvement."

As much of a jerk as it made him, he was about to use that little fact to his advantage. The idea that had teased him earlier now fell firmly into place.

As he looked into her cautious gaze, Paxton kept his expression serious. It would be all too easy to slip into charming-businessman mode, like he had with Auntie. That realm he could navigate easily. But Ivy would feel like she was being played.

He needed her on board. Not on edge.

"Ivy, I want to come stay with you."

The shock that widened her eyes reverberated inside of Paxton. He couldn't believe he was saying it out loud. But this made the most sense to him…and he hadn't been able to come up with a better option to get the amount of information he needed.

Thankfully she didn't mock his motives, or rage about the time they'd spent apart. Instead she seemed almost sad as she whispered, "Why?"

"We're having a baby together."

"Not really," she countered. "I mean, we have created a child together. But we aren't really together, are we?"

She had a point. Paxton stood, the need to clarify his thoughts pushing him to pace. "No," he said. As uncomfortable as it might be, they needed to get this point out in the open. "For now, we aren't together." He pivoted to face her. "But we will always be tied to one another. And right now, I'd say I know as little about you outside of work as you know about me."

She was already shaking her head. "I just can't deal with this right now, Paxton. Maybe later—"

"That's just it. I've had a lot of experience with pregnant women. You know that." After all, she'd watched him go to appointment after appointment with his sister last year, when her husband was away on business. "Auntie says Jasmine wants her to go on a trip with them. Let me take care of you. It will be easier on you, and on—"

"How's it going in here?" Auntie asked as she came back through the door with a tea tray. She set it on a little table near the couch. "Here's some ginger tea, sweetheart. Sip this slowly."

She handed a delicate teacup to Ivy, who raised it to her lips for a little sip before saying, "Thank you, Auntie."

The older woman limped over to a recliner, then lowered herself into it gingerly. Ivy frowned as she watched, the questions obvious on her face.

"Actually, Auntie," Paxton said, taking a chance despite the growing horror in Ivy's expression, "I'm trying to convince Ivy to let me stay here for a while. Let me take care of her. Take the burden off you so you can go on the trip with Jasmine."

Auntie glanced at Ivy with an almost-amused expression that he didn't understand. "Now, young man, don't you use me to put pressure on this young lady. She's carrying enough guilt as it is."

"I didn't mean to—"

"Then you don't know women as well as you think you do," she said with a smile. "Most women feel guilty for something or other. Ivy has had to take a step back lately, let other people do the work while her body handles the process of creation. That's not what she's used to…but I do think you have a point."

"You do?" Paxton hadn't thought she'd come on-board without some persuasion.

"This isn't really about me," Auntie chided him with a soft smile. "It's about you and Ivy. And you can't figure out anything about you and Ivy without working it out together." She transferred her smile to the woman looking pale and panicked on the couch. "It's hard to do that with distance...and a chaperone."

A stubborn expression took up residence on Ivy's face. "So you want to let someone you don't know live here while you're gone?"

"But you know me, don't you, Ivy?" Paxton prompted.

"So why did you accuse me of getting pregnant on purpose? Obviously you don't know me."

Paxton gave in to the renewed desire to pace. He didn't want to get into the particulars of his doubts, his accusations. But he wasn't seeing a way out. Especially not with Auntie's and Ivy's gazes trained directly on him. The pressure to explain warred with the desire to be defensive about his mistakes. "It was a long time ago."

"Did someone try to trap you into marriage?" Ivy asked, her wide eyes a sign of surprise he didn't believe.

Auntie made a soft clucking sound of comfort.

"No," Paxton assured her. Veronica hadn't trapped him into anything. "I have simply been deceived in the past by women who want more than I care to give. While I don't think that's what's happening here, the question had to be asked."

Auntie laughed. "Son, if someone is scamming you, I doubt they're just gonna admit it when you ask directly like that. But I can assure you, my niece is on the up-and-up. Besides, I doubt she was the one who brought the birth control to the party. Right?"

"Auntie!" Ivy cried, her pale cheeks flushing rose-red.

Paxton would normally have chuckled, but he was too lost in the memory of grabbing a condom from the bedside table. The box of condoms he'd bought. She was right. Birth control was always something Paxton handled himself. Only this time it had failed him.

He felt a low throb in his body, as if reminding him it had all been worth it. Too bad his body lied.

Then Ivy pressed a hand to her stomach and grimaced. As she lifted the teacup back to her lips, Paxton decided to give her some breathing room. Normally, he pressed hard when he wanted something. Pressed until he received the answer he wanted. But now wasn't the time for that…and he had a feeling Ivy wasn't a woman who would take it.

"Look, just think about it. I think it would be good for us." Even if maintaining his distance would be harder under those circumstances. But he had to remember his life plan. This might be a detour, but he refused to be derailed from his own goals. Or his family's expectations. "I'll come by tomorrow."

"Why don't you just call?" Ivy asked.

Maybe he would press…just a little more. "Because regardless of your decision, you're stuck with me. Yours is only a choice of location."

Four

"Auntie, why didn't you tell me?"

Ivy hated the whine in her voice, but couldn't seem to suppress it. Every minute that brought her closer to having Paxton staying with her, in her house, alone together…well, her nerves were definitely on edge. She'd just found out that he was due to arrive in a few hours and would be staying for the duration of Auntie's trip with Jasmine.

"Unlike Paxton," Auntie said with a small smile, "I know how women work emotionally. There's no need for you to feel responsible for my decision to have him stay here."

Ivy glanced at Jasmine as they crowded around her bed in the far upper room of the house. "Really?"

Ivy said. Jasmine had been just as bad, keeping their plans quiet until the last minute.

Her sister shrugged. "Not my place to tell you we were going, either," she said. "Stop with the grumpy face."

"Don't I have a say?" Ivy asked, throwing her hands up in a futile gesture. "I'm a grown woman, perfectly capable of taking care of myself."

"Not right now, you aren't," Auntie said. As she walked through the door, she threw back over her shoulder, "And guess what? That's okay."

No. It never was, in her book.

The energy drained from her, causing Ivy to plop down on the bed. "Am I doing the right thing?"

Both of Ivy's sisters paused in sorting the laundry on her bed to stare at her. Unable to handle the astonishment in their looks, she turned away. She let her nervous fingers trace the hand-sewn stitches on the quilt Auntie had made for her for her eighteenth birthday. "I'm not myself, okay?"

"You must not be," Willow said with an astonished tone. "Because I've never known you to ask us what the right choice is."

"Ever," Jasmine agreed.

Willow chuckled. "You keep this up, we might start to think you're human."

Ivy grimaced. It wasn't so much that she thought she knew everything. She simply hated to burden other people with her problems, or her upkeep, or her needs or wants. She preferred to give rather than receive...ever since her parents had died and she'd found herself as the youngest child with everyone else struggling to support her.

As her brain entered yet another round of asking, *What am I going to do about Paxton*? She wilted. No nausea so far today, but her entire body felt drained. Hopefully the doctor had been right and she only had a little over a month of this to go. Then her hormones would calm down and the nausea would subside.

She could feel her sisters' gazes on her, their concern, which was why they'd come over to help Auntie pack and get some things straightened up before their trip. But she wasn't sure how to express herself right now. This baby seemed to have sucked the life from her brain, as well as her body.

She also suspected they wanted to check out the situation firsthand, make sure she wasn't being forced to do something she didn't want to do. Or that Paxton wasn't even more volatile than the last row they'd seen, even though Ivy had assured them that that was unusual for him.

Jasmine tried to reassure her. "You don't have to do this if you don't want to. Even if he's already at the door. We'll figure it out."

And leave Auntie disappointed that she couldn't go with Jasmine and her daughter, Rosie, on this special trip. "I'm scared not to," Ivy whispered.

That had them dropping the laundry and closing in. "Why?"

Jasmine grabbed one of her hands. "We'll simply stay home if this is too much. You know we'll do everything in our power to take care of you."

Which was exactly what Ivy didn't want. Her sisters both had their hands full these days. The last thing Ivy wanted to be to anyone was a burden.

She rubbed her palm over her lower belly. As much as this little booger was giving her fits, she loved it already. Sight unseen. "I know that. But I need to do this… There's a lot at stake."

Her sisters scooted closer. Jasmine draped an arm around her shoulders. "Are you gonna tell him?" she asked.

Ivy knew what they meant. The secret history their family shared with Paxton's. The history he didn't even know about. Oh, he'd heard the story, of course. Probably many times, considering it was one of his ancestors who had died when her family allegedly sabotaged one of his family's most impressive cargo ships several generations ago. It had sunk off the coast of Savannah, with the family's heir inside.

Her family had been accused of destruction of property and murder. There wasn't any proof, but that hadn't stopped the McLemores from destroying her great-grandfather's life anyway, until he'd had to move away to protect the safety of his wife and daughter.

Only, he'd been innocent all along.

Jasmine had thought she was safe. After all, the family name had died with their mother. Their return to live with Auntie after their parents' deaths went unnoticed by anyone aware of the tragedy. There had been no reason for Paxton to ever know his employee was hiding her true identity from him.

Now she was tangled up in a web that felt deceitful, even though she'd never meant it that way. Despite the beliefs of Paxton's family, her great-grandfather had been a good man. But she had no way to prove his innocence at the moment. Ivy raised her gaze to Jasmine's worried expression. "What are the odds of us raising a child together without him ever finding out who I really come from?" she asked.

Well, they wouldn't be truly together…not in the way she'd dreamed of before that magical night. But they would still talk, interact with each other, make decisions together, right? Now that she knew for certain Paxton would be a part of her child's life, Ivy knew it would be important to stay on good terms with him.

As much as that was within her power.

Her stomach lurched for the first time today. This was not how she'd imagined having a child, nor how she'd imagined being with Paxton.

"I'm sorry," Willow said. "Maybe soon I will have the proof we need. That's why I went to Sabatini House, to see if I could find proof that the Sabatini pirates were actually responsible for sinking that ship, but I got a little distracted."

Willow rubbed her own belly then. Her sister had found herself pregnant only a few weeks after Ivy. But her circumstances were much different…and happier. Ivy reassured her, "What you found there was far more important than family history."

"Hopefully we'll have the pieces we need to prove our family's innocence soon enough," Jasmine said.

"Should we have a plan?" Willow asked.

Ivy frowned as unease drifted through her body. "That seems wrong…devious, somehow."

"Why?" Willow asked. "It's called contingency planning. There are certain things you can't control, but we need to decide ahead of time if there are circumstances where you need to give the details of our family history. Otherwise, the best plan is silence. For now."

"I can't think of any reason you would bring this up yourself," Jasmine said with a shake of her head. "I think the plan should just be silence, unless he brings it up himself."

"How would he find out?" Ivy asked.

Willow snorted in a very unladylike fashion. "Who knows? Then again, you don't really know Paxton very well outside of work, do you?"

Ivy was ashamed to admit that she didn't, although she had felt like she did. Day in and day out in each other's company had given her a false sense of familiarity. But she'd kept it that way on purpose. While she'd fantasized about more, she'd never planned on getting closer to Paxton than watching him from across his desk. For this very reason. She'd needed a good paying job…and he was never supposed to know who she really was.

"No, I don't," she mumbled. "I definitely can't tell him anything until I know more about him and his family."

"Then focus on that," Jasmine said. "Besides, connecting with him on a deeper level will be very valuable if his family disapproves later on."

Ivy really didn't want to think about that. Paxton's

family had never been very friendly when she'd seen them in the office. They pretty much pretended she wasn't there unless they needed something. It didn't take a genius to realize that her past wouldn't be the only problem with that crew. Her present circumstances would throw up just as strong of a roadblock.

Willow added as they stood to go downstairs, "That will give me time to do my thing. I'll see if I can find any more connections as we work on cleaning out the attic, too."

That would be good. The attic at Sabatini House had yielded the first answer the girls had looked for about their past. The sisters grinned at one another. Ivy's stomach settled once more. Though she worked really hard to be independent, her family was the best support a woman could ever ask for.

As she made her way downstairs with her sisters, she felt calm for the first time since she'd known Paxton was coming to stay with her.

"See," Willow went on. "I think this is a very solid contingency plan."

Paxton's voice shot at them from the doorway at the other end of the hall. "And why would you need one of those?"

Paxton hadn't been expecting a landing party when he'd shown up at the Harden place to take care of Ivy. The sea of people now crowded into the front parlor would have been intimidating for anyone not used to addressing groups like he was… In truth, he found himself energized by the challenge.

He recognized Ivy's sisters from the pictures that used to be on her desk at work, along with the sweet little toddler with dark curly hair in Jasmine's arms. Ivy's niece, Rosie.

The sole man in the group he recognized for a completely different reason. His presence was a bit of a shock. Ivy had never mentioned Royce Brazier to him. He'd heard through the grapevine when he'd returned home that Royce had recently become engaged to his event planner, but he'd had no reason to look into the details.

He'd only vaguely remembered Ivy's sister was an event planner. She had never been very forthcoming about her family at work.

As if drawn to the only other male in a sea of femininity, Paxton held out his hand. "Good to see you again, Royce."

"Long time, no see," Royce agreed.

His handshake was firm—firmer than usual. Though it had been almost a year since he'd interacted with him, Paxton didn't remember Royce as the type to pull macho power plays. But the look that accompanied the move assured Paxton that Royce was the person in charge here.

"All right," he said as he released Paxton's hand. "Let's give the man some room to breathe."

Auntie waved her arms around in a shooing motion to disperse the crowd from the front room. Suddenly the rapt audience began fiddling with luggage and discussing itineraries. The noise faded as they finished their last-minute preparations.

Only then did Paxton realize that Ivy wasn't there. Had she not been in the room all along? Had she snuck out while the rest of the family was piling in?

Nobody mentioned her absence as they rushed into last-minute preparations for their trip. In the sea of scurrying women, Paxton and Royce stood still.

As he continued to watch the strangely coordinated movements, a tingle of panic rose inside Paxton. Where was Ivy? Was something wrong?

Oblivious to the other man now, Paxton took a step toward the doorway, determined to find out where she'd gone. Only to have Royce move directly into his path.

Paxton took a deep breath, forcing himself to relax, not to let the other man see his hackles rise at the move.

"Is something wrong?" he asked.

"No," Royce said, though his deliberate stance belied the casual denial. Arms crossed over his chest. Legs braced. Definitely in charge. "Not at all."

Paxton raised a brow in inquiry, waiting to see where Royce wanted this conversation to go. He didn't have to wait long.

"I just thought it would be a good idea to make sure we're all on the same page before most of Ivy's family travels across the country, leaving her alone with a man none of us know very well."

The suspicion in his voice was blatant. Not that Royce was attempting to hide it.

"Royce, that's not really necessary." Paxton reminded himself he would probably issue his own warnings over his sisters and pushed down the rising need to fight for the alpha-male position. "You've met me before. You're aware of my reputation. Do you really think I'd hurt her?"

"This isn't professional—it's personal. And each of these women has come to mean a lot to me." Royce's gaze didn't waver from his for a minute. "I think every woman deserves someone to look out for her, to back her up."

"I agree."

Royce continued to study him for a moment longer than was comfortable. "I see you do. Just don't forget that Ivy's not alone in this. She might not like the idea, but we are here for her nonetheless."

Regardless of that last cryptic sentence, Paxton totally got that Ivy now had the backing of not just any man, but one of the most powerful men in Savannah. As much as Paxton liked to think of his family as loving, they were also business people, who more often than not made decisions based on logic and profitability, rather than emotions.

It was a reputation they'd carefully cultivated; it was also the truth. Looking at it in that light, Paxton saw clearly Royce's need to protect Ivy.

"I understand."

"I don't think you do," Royce said, for the first time breaking into a grin. "But you will." He patted Paxton's shoulder as he urged him toward the hall. "Just remember—I've been there. The learning curve is steep, but oh so worth it."

Huh?

As the two men headed into the hall that ran the

length of the house, Paxton thought back to the swirling rumors he'd paid little attention to at the family dinner when his sisters had tried to catch him up on all he'd missed while he was out of town. The only reason he'd listened was because he never knew when a bit of gossip could lead to a business breakthrough.

Had the stone-cold businessman finally grown a heart? From what Paxton could read, he had—at least for the Harden sisters.

But Paxton had always had a heart, hadn't he? Even when he chose to work strictly based on logic instead.

"Where did Ivy go?" he asked as they moved into the long hallway that ran the length of the house.

"I'm pretty sure she's back here," Royce said as he led the way to the kitchen.

Sure enough, Ivy sat at the table, surrounded by women who chatted and filled the room with last-minute admonishments to take care of herself.

Auntie beamed as they walked inside. "She ate some broth."

"Now, if I can keep it down," Ivy said in a snarky tone that Paxton wasn't used to hearing from her.

But she seemed to shake it off as she stood up for hugs all around and an extra kiss for Rosie. "Y'all have a good time," she said.

Though her expression was cheerful, Paxton suspected it was forced for their benefit. If he hadn't been watching her instead of the mass exodus going on around them, he would have missed the momentary droop, the dropping of her guard that allowed him to briefly glimpse the exhaustion underneath the facade. Luckily her family didn't seem to see it.

He knew in that moment how very important it was to her that her family see her as strong. Capable. Had this ordeal been difficult for her? Forced her to concede a weakness she would rather have kept hidden? Required her to lean on them?

Her discomfort about being dependent probably extended to him, too, considering the speed with which her mask reappeared. Almost before he could even blink, he faced a sphinx instead of the warm, professional woman he was more familiar with.

He was even less prepared when she turned immediately back down the hall after closing the door behind her family. "I'm going to lie down now," she said.

Paxton trailed after her as she made her way slowly up the stairs. To his amusement, that seemed to make her pick up her pace.

"Is there anything I can get you?" he asked, while doing his level best to ignore the firm curve beneath the soft pants she wore.

She didn't pause before opening a door about halfway down the hall. Paxton had a brief glimpse of silk and lace and a mixture of pastel and vibrant colors. No halfway for Ivy. He felt like it was a momentary glance of the woman behind the professional facade.

Very quickly she turned back to him, pulling the door closed until he could only see her face. "I'll catch you later," she said, then shut the door almost on his nose.

So much for reconnaissance.

Five

Ivy jumped at the sharp knock on her bedroom door.

"Dinner."

Paxton's tone brooked no argument. After Ivy had refused lunch, it wasn't surprising. She'd been locked in her room all day—napping, reading and completely ignoring Paxton. Even if she did pause at every noise, her throat tightening as she wondered if he would try her door.

Guess he reached his limit.

So had she. Though worried it would make her nauseous, she knew she needed to eat.

Just walking into the kitchen made her mouth water. She couldn't tell what it was exactly, but the heavenly smell seemed to make her feel warm and cozy all by itself. Paxton looked up from the pot on the stove.

"Hungry?"

Her stomach growled as if it knew she wouldn't answer honestly if left to her own devices.

Paxton gave her a half grin that made her heart feel funny. "I'd say that's a yes," he said.

Anxious for something to distract her from his golden good looks, Ivy moved toward the cabinets to get plates. Then she noticed bowls already sitting on the counter. "Soup?" she asked, awkwardness stiffening her movements.

He nodded. "Have a seat."

"I can do—"

He didn't argue, but simply stepped into her path. "I said, sit."

She wanted to be angry, but he wasn't being rude. Just firm. Her treacherous body complied, melting into the nearest chair.

His busyness gave her the chance to admire his agile movements as he dished up the food and brought bowls to the table. Paxton had always moved with an almost languid lack of speed. He was never in a hurry, no matter how urgent the cause, but he always got the job done.

Steam rose from the bowls that he set on each of their place mats, tempting her to inhale. They were joined by perfect slices of cornbread. Could this man do anything wrong? This meal couldn't have been better designed to settle her stomach. Carbs and more carbs.

Not that her admiration sat well with her. She

wished she could ignore how capable he was, both in business and with people. Feeding her anger and resentment would make this situation a whole lot easier. Those emotions helped her keep him at arm's length, whereas admiration just made her want him more.

To hide her conflict, she leaned over the bowl and breathed deep. Potato. She remembered it as one of his favorite options this past winter from one of the local restaurants where she ordered his lunches. Paxton also set a tray on the table with little bowls of cheese, bacon, sour cream, ham and scallions.

"This is very domestic," she said. Almost immediately she winced, because she hadn't meant to sound petulant.

"Man cannot live by restaurant alone," he joked, ignoring her tone and flashing that grin again. "Not even the single man."

Ivy knew her mouth had fallen open, and she struggled to close it even though the surprise remained. "You made this?" she asked, remembering all the lunches she'd provided to him over the last year and a half. Paxton didn't believe in brown-bagging it.

He raised a brow. "Your extreme surprise is not very flattering."

She met his expression with a lifted brow of her own. "I think I have a right to be surprised. I used to order all your takeout, remember?" She gestured toward the steaming food. "I just assumed this came from a restaurant."

"No restaurant. Just these two hands." He raised

them, palms facing her, as if that alone would prove the truth.

She knew just how capable those hands were. In the office. With his family. In the bedroom. But she'd never guessed that they were also talented in the kitchen. Deep down inside, she was ashamed that she hadn't known this about a man whom she felt so deeply for. What other things about him did she not know outside of work?

For lunch, he ate at his restaurant of choice. Either there or had it delivered to the office. It never occurred to her that he was cooking like this at home. She stared down at the creamy concoction in her bowl.

"Though I do admit," he went on, as if conceding her point, "I had the groceries delivered."

Man, that grin was so hard to resist. As if sensing that she might be open to conversation now, he quickly changed the subject. "I've been looking around the house this afternoon."

There was a subtle accusation in his pointed glance that she chose to ignore. "This house has excellent craftsmanship. Have you always lived here?" he continued.

Without thinking, Ivy answered, "Auntie's family built it. Then she and her husband lived here during their marriage."

Paxton's brow furrowed...the first sign of her mistake. "I'm confused," he said.

Shoot. How much could she say without saying too much? "Oh, Auntie isn't really our aunt. She took us girls in when my parents died."

"Wow." Paxton looked impressed. "She went from no children to three girls? That's a very big sacrifice. I assume she knew your parents well?"

Certainly Ivy was aware of the dangerous waters she was swimming in. Any discussion of her family or Auntie's family could move into dangerous territory very quickly, so she'd keep her answers short and sweet. "She was my mother's nanny."

She took a couple more bites as an excuse to not talk.

"I didn't know you were an orphan. How did your parents die?"

Ivy's stomach twisted. Her parents' deaths were not something she was comfortable discussing, even after all these years. "It was a car accident," she choked out.

The flash of grief, memories of a young child devastated at the sudden loss, made her antsy. She found herself crumbling the last bite of cornbread on her plate between her thumb and forefinger.

"Were y'all from here? Originally?" he asked.

The questions seemed so innocent, but were they? Ivy's emotions coalesced into a distinct unease. Until she found the right path, she had to protect her family.

Oblivious, Paxton went on. "There definitely seems to be a sailing theme around here." He pointed to some of the memorabilia in the china cabinet, a few ships in miniature that had been passed down to the girls. "Was your family in the shipping business?"

Alarm sped through Ivy with the speed of a wildfire. She stared deep into her empty bowl, wishing she had more of the yummy goodness. Not because she was hungry, but just to have something to occupy her hands. "I'd really rather not talk about this right now," she mumbled.

Then she forced herself to her feet and carried her bowl across to the stove.

"Let me do that," Paxton insisted, rising from his seat.

"I can do it."

It was ridiculous how often she had to repeat that these days. She was capable, though some days she needed to convince herself that she *could* do things, even if it was something as simple as fixing herself a bowl of soup.

"I don't mind," he said. "Let me do it for you."

Helplessness washed over her, but she refused to give in. *Stubborn.* It's what her family had always called her. Through clenched teeth, she repeated, "I can do it, Paxton. I'm not an invalid."

The strength of her emotions washed away any desire for more food. Embarrassment filtered into the mix. But she hated anyone thinking she was weak, hated how much she had to rely on other people these days.

But most of all, she hated how out of control everything felt...

This reconnaissance mission is going nowhere.

Frustration sharpened Paxton's nerves as he stared out the window late that night. He couldn't even focus on the laptop open before him. Concentrating on work had never been a problem. This situation was just unusual enough to cause a simmering mixture of unease and frustration that blocked his usual productivity.

His purpose in coming here had been thwarted by one prickly blonde woman. Instead of hanging out together, or even sitting in the same room, Ivy had retreated to her bedroom not long after dinner—and he'd counted himself lucky that she'd hung around that long.

Though they had technically been in the same room, she'd pretended to sleep between lunch and dinner. She might actually have slept for a bit in front of the television, which was tuned to a marathon of a crazy reality show she hadn't seemed to be watching. He'd wondered more than once if she'd chosen it on purpose just to annoy him.

But what annoyed him more was that Ivy had refused to ask for anything to drink, had refused to let him fix her another bowl of soup, had refused to let him make her cookies.

What pregnant woman refused cookies?

But it was as if she had to prove to him that she didn't need him there at all. That she could get what she needed herself, rather than let him lend a hand.

Finally Paxton gave in and retired to the guest room for some sleep. He wasn't getting any work done, so he might as well call it a night. But the resolve wasn't enough to allow him to fall asleep. Instead he stared at the pressed-tin ceiling, wondering how to break through Ivy's insistent need for independence. About fifteen minutes passed before he heard footsteps upstairs. Slow steps, then running.

A door slammed. Paxton sat up to listen. Water

rushed through the pipes overhead. The sink? A toilet? He couldn't be sure.

That was the only sound for a few minutes, then he heard a loud thump. He jumped out of bed, his body preparing for action. What was that?

But the water continued to run, long enough that he wondered if she was taking a shower. His muscles relaxed as the water finally ceased.

Then the barest creak of a door. No footsteps. He cocked his head to the side, listening hard. Was she just standing there? Or tiptoeing down the hall? Then another heavy thud came. Almost directly overhead.

After that, nothing. Silence descended, aside from the normal household hum. What was she doing up there?

His heartbeat sped up a notch. A lot of *what-ifs* sped through his mind... But the fact that he couldn't distinguish between the normal household sounds and what could be a serious situation made him angry.

He didn't care if she wanted help or not. He was going. It only took a second to pull a pair of sweatpants over his boxers and make his way up the stairs two at a time, turning on lights to illuminate the dark of the house along the way.

The first thing he saw in the upper hall as the light flicked on was tangled blond hair spread across the green floor runner. For a moment time froze.

"Ivy!"

She lifted her head a little as he knelt beside her.

"I'm fine," she said, but her voice was thready. Though she normally maintained the gorgeous porcelain skin of a Southern belle, right now she had the sickly-gray cast of someone definitely under the weather.

"Obviously." For the moment, his fear was easier to handle as sarcasm. But beneath the coping mechanism, he could feel rage building. "So, lying on the floor is just more comfortable than your bed?"

She patted the runner beneath her. "Just looking for a change of scenery."

"You know my room is directly below this spot, right?"

She closed her eyes, but he wasn't letting her ignore him this time.

"All you had to do was call my name. Heck, say my name and I would probably have heard you." Heat slipped into his voice without permission, but dammit, why hadn't she just called him for help?

He didn't think any further, didn't ask what she needed. He simply swept her up in his arms. She shrieked, but he ignored her.

"Put me down!"

Pretending to comply, he let her legs sweep down until her feet touched the floor, then lifted his arms in a hands-off gesture…until she swayed. "Sure that's what you want?" he asked.

A whimper was the only answer he waited for, before he picked her back up and strode down the hall to her room.

It wasn't until he set her onto the bed that he registered the bare skin against his palms. As he stepped back, the disheveled covers and hair reminded him

of a much more titillating scenario. Something that shouldn't be registering at this point. He quickly pulled his mind back from the brink and focused in on his anger. That seemed the safer, easier option.

"Are you really so angry with me that you'd rather sleep on the floor than ask for help?" He exploded, giving the frustration free rein. "And why were you on the floor in the first place?"

Ivy covered her face. At first he thought she was simply avoiding his demanding questions. "This resistance to any bit of help is getting very childish, Ivy."

Then her shoulders started to shake. Paxton realized she wasn't blocking him out. She was crying.

"No—wait."

He held out both hands as if to pat her shoulders, but pulled back at the last minute. He wanted answers, but not like this. Upsetting her was the last thing he wanted. He hated for his sisters to cry. It made him feel helpless. But when Ivy lifted her face, *helpless* didn't begin to describe his emotions.

"You don't understand!" she spat out. "Two months ago, I was a fully functioning, fully capable woman. Now I have no job. No life. And apparently no ability to walk, either!"

Paxton could only stare as tears continued to rush over her cheeks.

"I'm just tired and weak and disgusting. Half the time, I can't fix myself something to eat. I'm too exhausted to work. I haven't done my nails in weeks. I mean, look at my hair!"

It was a genuine feminine complaint in the midst of

bigger issues. Paxton understood. Her words painted a better picture of the loss of control she was feeling right now. His brain latched on to the details as something he could finally fix, something he could do to actually improve her feelings about this situation, as opposed to simply covering the basics.

But he had a feeling she wasn't going to like his next move, either.

Six

The feelings washing over Ivy were even more out of control than her usual pregnancy doldrums. *Why had she been cursed with hormones?* Though that was probably a common female lament at various times in life, in this moment it was her truly heart-felt cry. Without consent, tears overflowed her eyes and trailed down her cheeks, even as she cursed her weakness.

This time she didn't protest as Paxton once again lifted her into his arms and retraced his steps down the hall. His destination: the bathroom where she'd just gotten sick. Her ill-fated attempt to make it back to her bedroom on her own, even though she'd known she was weak, had ended with her collapsing on the floor.

Even now her limbs felt weighted with the heaviness of fatigue. Her eyes refused to open. She was too tired to fight, too overwhelmed to keep her emotions under wraps. The roller coaster of the last three months was now running off the rails.

Heat burned beneath her skin as she remembered her whining complaints. At least, that's probably how Paxton heard them. Without comment he set her on the stool they kept in the good-sized room, then moved away. It wasn't until she heard water running into the tub that she started paying attention. Her soggy eyelashes took an effort to lift. "What are you doing?"

He didn't even look up from his task. "You'll be more comfortable if we wash you up."

"We?" she squeaked.

"You just collapsed on the floor. Are you gonna do this alone?"

She felt her mouth open to defend herself, but nothing came out. She glanced at the water, able to almost feel the heat with the rising steam. Then she looked back at the larger-than-life male pulling fluffy towels from the cabinet. Tendrils of sensual awareness shimmered through her exhaustion—familiar even though distant.

No. No. No.

She was not getting naked in front of him again.

Then he poured some of her favorite bubble bath into the running water. The soft sent of bourbon sugar filled the air. Her muscles started to ache, as if demanding to be immersed in the liquid warmth. Her body desperately wanted to relax, to rest…along with her brain.

Paxton used her distraction to his advantage. With a rush of fabric, her oversize T-shirt was whisked over her head, leaving her clad in nothing but her underclothes. Only then did she realize just how much of the lower half of her body had been on display. Even more was on display now.

"In you go," he said like a nursemaid, urging her to her feet so that she was facing the tub.

At least she didn't have to watch his expression while he undressed her. But that didn't stop the worries from rushing in. Unaware of her runaway thoughts, he popped open the clasp on her bra, and part of her wondered if he was just no longer interested in her…sexually.

Why couldn't she shut down these distressing thoughts?

Especially when his warm fingers brushed her hips as he pushed her panties down. Almost immediately a towel was draped over her shoulders.

He's protecting my modesty, not ogling. Why did that thought depress her? Contrary tears prickled the backs of her eyes. She didn't want to be wanted just because she was a naked woman.

Any naked woman.

But his practical touch reinforced the fact that he no longer saw her as desirable—just as the mother of his child. Someone he would take care of, but not cherish the way she'd dreamed of months before.

Ivy squeezed away the tears and focused on the

warmth of the water as he guided her gently over the edge, into the tub. As she sank beneath the bubbles into sheer bliss, she heard him close the curtain.

A weird mixture of disappointment and relief shimmered through her. She saw his shadow lower as he sat on the stool. Trying to ignore the intimacy of the moment, she let her eyes close once more and focused on the sweet-scented steam in the air, the lap of water against the sides of the bathtub, and the loosening of her muscles in the liquid heat.

"Any more nausea?" Paxton finally asked.

Ivy did a quick self-check and realized her body was settling down, even if her mind wasn't. "No," she answered simply.

"Okay… Just give me a little warning if need be."

That was funny. "I'll give you as much warning as I'm given."

"I completely understand," he said with a chuckle.

Ivy lay cocooned in steamy warmth, lazily watching the bubbles float with her subtle movements, hyperaware of Paxton on the other side of the curtain. His silence. His vigilance.

"You've been pretty sick," he said, his tone deepening. "That must make the idea of motherhood pretty daunting."

"Not as much as doing it all alone." She immediately tensed, knowing she probably shouldn't have said that…but it was at least honest.

"You don't have to."

His quiet voice was steady, but could she trust

him? If only it were that simple. She couldn't hold back her answer. "I'm not so sure about that."

Outside the curtain, he shifted, causing the stool to squeak. "Look, I'm here. I'm staying."

Maybe it was time for her to address the elephant in the room. At least this situation helped her feel secure, facing him but not really having to see him through the curtain. First she took a deep breath; then she let it out.

"So, why didn't you stay before?"

No good deed went unpunished.

Paxton had simply assumed Ivy would avoid any kind of deep discussion now, the same way she had since he'd gotten here. Her question came out of the blue.

A dozen excuses ran through his head while his lungs struggled for air in the steamy space. *I'm not ready. I wasn't prepared for what happened. I wasn't sure I wanted this to continue. I don't want to know if what I'm feeling is more than lust...*

He couldn't say any of that...but she deserved something real. Paxton wasn't sure if it was the warm air, the soft scent of vanilla or the sounds from the bath that brought to mind images of Ivy's soft skin and even softer curves—whatever the cause, it loosened his tongue.

Maybe it had been the same for her, the intimate atmosphere prompting something deeper.

Without permission, he heard himself say, "I was afraid."

The silence that engulfed the room seemed to echo in his ears. His throat clenched in a belated attempt to hold the words inside. Why had he said that? What was he thinking?

He wasn't. In an attempt to cover up the truth, he rushed into speech. "I just didn't want to ruin our working relationship."

Yes, that sounded perfectly logical.

"We work—worked—so perfectly together, and I could trust everything was taken care of when I wasn't there. I didn't want to risk losing that."

Ivy wasn't buying it. "Since when do you run instead of facing problems head on?"

Ah, the joys of arguing with someone who knows you all too well.

"I wasn't running." *It was more of a strategic retreat.* "I had a business issue to attend to, and felt we should talk about it face-to-face."

"Sure, in a week or two... Not two months later."

Funny how he could picture her slightly affronted expression just from her tone of voice. "So, why didn't you bring it up?" he asked, not willing to accept all of the blame.

"And risk losing my job?"

He couldn't argue that. Though he did lose sight of it from time to time, he was very aware they were in a situation where he was the one with the power. And a lot of Ivy's choices had reflected that same knowledge.

"But didn't you walk away from it in the end, anyway?"

Her sigh sounded sad, defeated. "Yes," she conceded. "And it was one of the hardest decisions I've ever had to make."

While Paxton had simply avoided making any decision at all...until she'd forced him to with her actions.

"Do you know what I think?" she asked.

He wasn't sure he really wanted to know.

"I think you couldn't figure out how to handle me or what had happened between us. You had no perfect plan."

He grunted as her words hit home, but he wasn't ready to concede just how much their night together had impacted him. Not yet. Maybe a distraction would get him off the hook. "Let's get your hair washed before the water gets cold."

"I don't need help—"

"Right." He'd heard that a time or two. "Exactly how long do you think you can hold your hands over your head right now?"

Suddenly it was her turn for silence.

He couldn't suppress a grin. Victory, even a small one, felt pretty good. He let himself rub it in, just a little. "I thought so. And I know I heard you say your hair was driving you crazy. Don't worry... I've washed my nieces' hair plenty since they were babies."

Which was a load of bull, because he knew touching Ivy in any way would be nothing like those innocent experiences. Paxton sucked in a deep breath, bracing himself for wet, naked skin. When he pulled back the shower curtain, he found Ivy shifted forward, her arms wrapped around knees covered in bubbles.

The pose shouldn't have been provocative. All major erogenous zones were thoroughly covered by her arms or the thick bubbles drifting on the gentle current of the water. It was the bare curve of her spine, so vulnerable, so sexy, that had his breath catching in his throat. Not to mention the wealth of golden waves that spilled over each shoulder as if to frame the intimate sight.

He held up a shampoo bottle. "This one?"

She looked up briefly to confirm, then nodded at him. He picked up the large plastic cup nearby and used it to douse her hair with water. The long, tangled locks flattened instantly, spilling across her back to shield him from the tempting sight of her skin.

Paxton braced himself against the side of the bathtub. His body's response to seeing her like this was swift and immediate, like a kick in the gut. But instead of intense pain, intense pleasure shot through him.

Eager to avoid this response, he let it drive him into action. Though not the type of action he craved.

The liquid shampoo was cool and thick as he squeezed it into his palm. Another sweet vanilla scent, but it didn't quite match the bubble bath. He rubbed his palms together, spreading the mixture as he studied her hair and formulated a plan of attack. Finally he aimed for the wet mass right around her shoulders. He could feel the tangles as he rubbed in the shampoo. Even when wet, her hair was thick and heavy.

Not at all like the children's. Usually with them it was a couple of quick strokes and they were ready to rinse. Even when his oldest niece's hair had started growing in for real. Not this time.

His hands instinctively worked the shampoo into the thickness, down to the tips and then back up to the top. The mass seemed to grow under his attention, forcing him to corral it, rub it, scrub it.

That's when he heard the first tiny response. Small noises at first, slowly growing into deep moans as he worked his fingers against her scalp. So very similar to the sounds he had heard one special night before.

Rivulets of foamy shampoo bubbles spilled down onto her glistening skin, making it look slick and oh so touchable. Dangerous territory, his mind warned.

Inadvertently his thumbs pressed down the length of her neck, easing the tension in the muscles along her spine. A soft sigh of satisfaction had him freezing in place.

He didn't realize his hands had gone still against her head until she lifted it slightly. She didn't open her eyes, probably to keep the shampoo from getting into them. Regardless of the reason, he was relieved.

"Everything okay?" she asked, her voice now husky.

No! "Almost done."

He forced himself to view the task logically as he rinsed the soap from her hair, then added conditioner and ran a wide-tooth comb through the mass to remove tangles at her instruction.

But the wild feeling of satisfaction—the peace that stole over him, telling him there was nowhere else he'd rather be—wouldn't be washed away.

Seven

Consciousness came slowly to Ivy the next morning. She woke in a much more leisurely manner than her usual "shocked opening of her eyes, rush for the toilet" ritual of the last two months. Even so, she lay perfectly still, evaluating her body for any concerns. No nausea yet, but she was still hesitant to move. Often that would start the cycle in the morning if she didn't already feel like tossing her cookies.

After a good ten minutes, she lifted one eyelid to peek at the clock. Nine o'clock in the morning. The house around her was silent, but it wasn't the normal silence of people still sleeping. It was more of a feeling of emptiness, as if she were the only one in the building.

Paxton had let her sleep in? But was he still here

somewhere? She had a feeling that he was a consistently early riser, despite the middle of the night interruption he'd had.

Hopefully he had no idea just how she'd responded to his touch last night. The morning sickness of the last two and a half months had certainly done a number on her libido. But her body had forgotten all about that when his hands had been in her hair. She'd attempted to keep her outward response to an absolute minimum out of embarrassed modesty. After all, it was clear from his smooth touch and strict attention to her hair alone, not to mention his leaving after making sure she could safely get herself dried off and dressed, that he was no longer interested in her naked body. She just hoped she had adequately hidden the telltale tightening of her nipples and the ache that surely must have shown on her face.

It wasn't even just a desire for sex. The awakening realization that his touch alone was just as powerful had shaken her. Before last night, she hadn't been conscious of just how much she'd craved the comfort and care of his touch. The feel of his fingers working against her scalp. The gentle pull of the comb as he released the tangles in her hair. The press of his thumbs along the muscles of her neck, releasing the tension, easing the stiffness.

It had been the stuff of both nightmares and passionate dreams. And she had no intention of letting him know just how intensely she'd felt every brush of his fingers.

The sudden sound of a door closing downstairs

forced her to finally sit up. Though she had no desire to face Paxton in person with all of these emotions running rampant inside of her, she refused to let herself cower behind her fears.

Ivy's hormones might be making her slow at the moment, but she was still a smart woman. She knew deep down that ignoring Paxton here in her house was not going to help her or her baby. Acting off emotions was not going to get her anywhere. Or at least not anywhere she wanted to go.

Time to wise up.

Her emotional side wanted to return Paxton to the role of lover. But that was not the reality of this situation.

She needed to think about the baby. And the future. Not the past.

Besides, she was just becoming aware of the stirring of hunger deep in her belly…miracle of miracles. Now that she knew he could cook—and cook really well—she had to wonder what he might have made for breakfast. Memories of his potato soup were like a warm, comfy blanket.

Getting dressed and the trek downstairs went well enough. She reached the bottom of the steps without feeling any nausea rising up the back of her throat. She sighed in relief, mentally tallying how many days she had until the doctor said she'd be out of the woods.

Of course there were no guarantees, but she sincerely hoped she was one of the lucky women who left morning sickness behind in the first trimester.

Since she obviously hadn't been lucky enough to not have it at all, like Willow.

Just the thought had her crossing all of her fingers and toes.

She found Paxton at the kitchen counter. She paused just outside the doorway so she could take in the sight of him chopping vegetables, the muscles in his shoulders rippling beneath his polo shirt as he moved. Inwardly she sighed in regret that nothing about this gorgeous picture would ever truly be hers, but she refused to let any of that show on the outside. Instead she forced herself to step through the doorway and say a quiet good morning.

"Good morning!" he replied over his shoulder.

Man, would she ever reach the point where she didn't have to steal herself against that charming grin? Or ask herself if it was really meant for her or just an automatic reaction to the world around him?

"I wasn't sure how you'd feel this morning," he said. He gestured toward a small plate of crackers on the table, and the tea cozy nestled next to it. "I picked up some more ginger tea for you."

Ivy eased into the seat, his thoughtful errand softening the armor she'd slowly been rebuilding since last night.

"I feel pretty good this morning, but better safe than sorry."

Pulling the cozy off, she lifted the warm cup to hold between her palms. The spicy ginger scent teased her senses. She watched him as she took a few cautious sips, then a couple of nibbles of the crackers.

Paxton expertly transferred the vegetables he was chopping to a frying pan without spilling any. Even the sizzle sounded delicious as the scent of butter filled the air. Then he began to crack eggs into a bowl.

The silence between them felt awkward after the intimacy of the night before. Though the words they'd spoken hadn't been comfortable or exactly what she'd wanted to hear, they had been honest. Only, now she didn't really know what to say to him face-to-face. How did she start rebuilding a bridge when she wasn't even sure what it looked like? How did one go about turning someone from a lover to something different? Something practical, like a co-parent.

Especially when everything inside of her ached for what might have been.

Finally she looked down at her plate and noticed a small tin next to it. "What's this?" she asked.

"I got those for you at the health food store this morning. I remembered one of my sisters mentioning how she swore by them when she was pregnant with her daughter. I figured it was worth a shot."

Inside the old-fashioned-looking tin, the little ginger lozenges were lined up in neat amber-colored rows. She lifted the tin to her nose. They smelled good. "Like you said, definitely worth a try."

"So, you seem to have learned a lot from them," she said, searching hard for that first plank on the bridge.

He nodded as he poured the egg mixture into the pan. "Watching them. Listening to them talk with my mom and grandmother. Reading articles about women and pregnancy. It helps to pay attention for those moments you can help...to make up for when you do screw up."

Ivy ignored the implication and let herself laugh as memories of his many internet searches came to mind. "You just love to learn about anything, don't you?"

He smiled sheepishly. "It doesn't matter if it's production or people—but my sisters deserve the best. I've been determined to give it to them."

She refrained from pointing out that that was probably the job of their husbands. Though she'd seen his sisters many times in his office, she'd never met their significant others. And she wouldn't have asked about them, even if given the chance.

Paxton's family, which he seemed to love to no end, was not necessarily a friendly lot. They rarely talked to her at work beyond the necessities of getting into Paxton's office, though by far Sierra was the most personable.

None of them seemed too big on seeing their employees as people, or at least not nearly as much as Paxton did. He was well loved within the company, and could often be found chatting with various employees in the hallways. Not just the upper management, but anyone from his secretary to an intern in the mail room.

He was rarely too busy for anyone.

"What will they think?" she asked cautiously.

Though they were just feeling their way now, eventually the news would spread. There would be no getting around that if Paxton planned to be a full-time part of the baby's life.

He didn't seem to catch her drift. "My sisters both love kids. Sierra has two. Alicia one. They'll be thrilled to have a cousin."

All her thoughts of allies and families pushed Ivy to ask, "What about me? Is that going to be a problem?"

Though Paxton paused to deliver a fully loaded omelet onto a plate and then place it on the table in front of her, Ivy knew there was a bit of a delay tactic in play. It took him more than a minute after setting the plate in front of her to actually meet her gaze, but to his credit, he did.

"I honestly don't know," he said.

Family was a complicated subject. How his family had treated her before wasn't something that was a credit to them, though his sisters were a bit more personable than his mother or grandmother. That woman scared the pants off Ivy.

But this was different.

Facing them alone scared Ivy. And her own family couldn't go with her everywhere, not even her new, overly protective big brothers in the form of her sisters' fiancés. She thought of her sisters' words from before…about the need to learn more about Paxton, learn how they could work together…so that she did have some form of buffer between her and his family.

She needed an ally. She looked at Paxton, who was across the table from her, digging into his omelet and toast. *A platonic ally.*

The words made her want to cry, but she forced herself to sit straighter and brace herself. No more attitude. No more overly emotional actions. The thought in and of itself brought sadness, not because she wanted to be ugly to him, but because she knew those emotions were just the flip side of the passion she'd felt before he'd abandoned her.

But for her baby's sake, she now needed someone who would stand by her side, help raise their child and form a united front against anyone who chose to tear apart their alliance.

Just no sex.

This isn't about romance, she reminded herself. This is about a joint effort to create an unconventional, but supportive family. She couldn't have the happily-ever-after, so she'd settle for whatever it was they were building right now.

"You're what?"

"We aren't coming home tomorrow."

Though Jasmine enunciated her words pretty well on the other end of the line, Ivy still wasn't comprehending. Maybe she didn't want to. Her time spent with Paxton had become more and more enjoyable. They had taken to playing games from the over-crowded wall of bookshelves in the front parlor, and talking about books and movies and plays. Subjects they'd never explored well within the confines of the office. Though part of it was Ivy doing her best to keep discussions of family and personal subjects to a minimum so she didn't accidentally give away anything she wasn't supposed to.

It was good. A good way to become allies, to get to know each other deeper than they had in their business relationship. But it had been hard on her personally. With Paxton right here, there was no break to nurse her feelings of sorrow and grief over the dreams she'd been forced to abandon.

"We want to add a little side trip," Jasmine was saying. "We're having such a good time, and we thought we would travel down into wine country and spend three or four days. Auntie is having so much fun, but she's really worried about you. Worried about leaving you for longer than we already have."

Well, that made Ivy feel good. *Not*. The last thing she wanted was for her family to worry over *her*.

"And it's so exciting, because Royce is giving up business to do this with us as a family. You know what a big deal that is."

Ivy did. Royce had been very much a button-down businessman before Jasmine got a hold of him. For him to just blow off business at the last minute? That would've been unheard of six months ago.

But deep down Ivy felt panic rising. She couldn't stay here for another week with Paxton. That wasn't fair to him. And she wasn't sure if she'd be able to keep her feelings to herself under those circumstances. He might spend an hour or two in front of the computer each day, but the rest of his time he devoted his attention to her. Under different circumstances it would have been a situation made in heaven.

But her current circumstances were not heavenly at all.

She drew in a breath, long and low. "Well, you can tell Auntie that I'm definitely improving. Between the ginger tea and the medicine from the doctor, and these little magic lozenges that Paxton brought me, I'm actually feeling great, keeping food down and regaining energy. I'm even feeling better enough to want to start sending out résumés again."

"Now Ivy, don't take on too much, too soon."

Ivy hated when her sister got that caretaker tone in her voice. Like she was too much of a child to make sound decisions. "I'm not. I'm just trying to do what I can, when I can."

The anger building in her chest was hard to suppress. So many people telling her what to do with her life was getting more than a little annoying.

Especially with all the uncertainty and unfavorable variables that kept popping up.

Digging deep, she forced a cheerful note. "But look, I'm thrilled that you're going to stay for a while. I don't want Auntie to worry. Everything is great." She hesitated for just a moment, then asked, "But can we just keep this information between ourselves?"

Caution entered Jasmine's voice. "What do you mean?"

"I mean…" she said, irritation quickly returning over the need to spell this out to someone she thought would understand. "Could we keep this between us? As in, could you please not tell Paxton about this?"

She'd handle that herself…once she figured out how.

"Don't tell me about what?"

Ivy whirled around to face Paxton, who had come in without her noticing. In his hand he held his phone at chest level, display facing her. The image showed a series of text messages with Royce's name at the top. The accompanying irritation on Paxton's face told her she'd made the wrong move. Again. She quickly said her goodbyes to Jasmine, along with even more assertions that everything would be fine.

Then she laid her phone on the table with a very careful movement and met that accusing gaze once more. "I'm sorry—"

"Is it really that horrible hanging out with me? Letting me take care of you? Why wouldn't you want me to know that your family is planning to stay gone another four days?"

She honestly hadn't been thinking about hurting his feelings. Just about handling this herself instead of imposing on Paxton even further. "When you put it that way, I know it sounds pretty bad."

He shook his head, some of the emotion draining from his expression. "No, I'm sure you have good reasons. It's just upsetting to know that we haven't come to a place where you would discuss them with me first."

That's actually what she'd wanted—after she'd had the chance to think through all of her reasoning. Guess she'd just have to wing it.

"Look, Paxton, I've used up a lot of your time and energy. Of everyone's, really. I just don't feel right taking up any more. You need to return to work. And to your family..."

Paxton looked away. Ivy knew exactly what he was thinking about. His mother had called several times during lunch on Sunday, until Paxton had finally answered. Apparently she had been extremely unhappy that he was not at the weekly family dinner, and he hadn't been willing to give her an excuse.

He'd been quiet and unsettled the rest of the afternoon.

Paxton paced back and forth, as if trying to get his thoughts gathered through movement. Such a familiar action that made her heart ache. "What if I could continue to help you and still do all those things?"

Ivy frowned. "What did you have in mind?"

She was already hiding out from his family and the world she'd known when she'd worked with him. How much more could she disappear?

Ivy wasn't very comfortable with how those thoughts made her feel. Selfish and jealous and just a little bit angry. Not pretty at all. And not necessary. She would never play a prominent part in Paxton's life again—she needed to get used to that idea.

Still she said, "I've used up everyone's time and energy—yours, my family's. That's hard for me. You need to return to work...to your life... I need... I don't know," she mumbled.

"Is there something I should be doing that I haven't?" The surprise in his voice was almost amusing.

"Paxton, what I need, neither you nor my family can give me." She might as well start being honest.

He just looked confused.

"I know it's hard to tell sometimes, especially right now." Her behavior had been less than exemplary. "But I'm very grateful for all the care and concern that everyone has given me. That doesn't mean it isn't hard for me to accept."

"Why?"

Though he'd asked, she thought she saw a glimmer of understanding in his gaze. Accusation was gone from his tone, leaving a genuine curiosity that she couldn't resist.

"Since my parents died, my sisters and Auntie have worked hard to keep our family afloat. We didn't always have much, but they worked hard for what we did have. I was little when Mom and Dad died. There wasn't much I could do to contribute. It made me feel…helpless."

The sounds he made were noncommittal, but his attentive gaze urged her to keep going.

"I've always pushed to be responsible for myself. I got my first real job when I was twelve years old. And now…" She gestured to her tummy. "I've made a stupid mistake," she whispered, closing her eyes against the welling tears she didn't want. Her push for independence had made her take the job with Paxton in the first place. She hadn't been able to resist the opportunity to make a good living. In a single night she'd jeopardized her ability to support herself and her family's reputation. "A mistake that's affected everyone. And I have to fix this."

"Not alone." Paxton's voice was closer than she'd expected.

Ivy opened her eyes just in time to see his arms enfolding her. It was the first time he'd held her since their one night together, and her treacherous body melted against him immediately.

He felt so good, warm and solid. Though she knew the security was an illusion, she couldn't resist it.

"You did not make that decision alone," he insisted. "You will not carry the consequences alone."

Paxton backed up to look down at her face, hands on her shoulders. "I know how capable you are. How driven. You're excellent at your job. That's why we work so well together." He shook his head. "But your work right now involves something you can't really see. Growing the baby inside of you—getting this pregnancy off on the right foot. It's a very special project—which means your other work has to be delegated for right now." He squeezed her shoulders gently. "Do you understand?"

For the first time, she really did. "But that doesn't change the fact that you still have other responsibilities, and family…" One she really did not want to know anything about her at the moment.

"You're right. I do." He paced away, leaving her feeling chilled without his touch. After a moment he swiveled back to face her.

"What if I could take care of you and the baby and still do all of those things, too?"

"And run yourself ragged?" She shook her head.

"I don't understand how that would work for either of us."

He turned to face her squarely, with that familiar posture she'd seen in the office many times. Arms crossed firmly over his chest. Legs wide and braced. She felt like she was being warned.

"It wouldn't require nearly as much effort...if you moved into my place."

Eight

Paxton took a deep breath as he circled the car to open Ivy's door. At least this was one part of their normal interactions that had stayed the same. Though she'd worked for him, any time they'd left the office together, he'd always made a point to treat her like a valued person and a lady. In the South, men opened doors for women as a courtesy. Though in truth, he'd often had women do the same for him.

But whenever possible, Paxton had always held the door for Ivy. Today the gesture felt familiar, a touchstone in a sea of constant changes. Paxton knew he was swimming out of his depth, even if he was convinced this was the right move.

He held out his hand, steadying her as she stood up. Luckily there'd only been a small hint of nausea on the ride over to his house. He hadn't been sure how she'd do in the car, even as smoothly as his car drove. But she seemed to be having a good day.

He smiled as he thought about the little ginger lozenges she was never without these days. At least he'd gotten that right.

She stared up at the stone facade and white trim of his two-story custom-built house as if dazzled.

"You've been here a couple of times before, right?" he asked.

Ivy glanced sharply in his direction before dropping her gaze. "Just once during the day. I dropped off some papers about a year ago, I believe."

And her other visit had been in the dark of night. That one, at least, Paxton wasn't likely to forget.

"We'll need to show you around when you're feeling up to it. I want to make sure you feel as at home as possible."

Her small smile was a weak concession. Her every hesitation, every refusal to meet his gaze broadcast her nerves. Paxton wished he knew how to break the ice better than this. Then again, he'd never brought a woman who was pregnant with his child home to live with him.

What could be more awkward under these circumstances?

He tried to view the surroundings from her perspective. The house was impressive, yes, but he'd bought it with the idea of raising a family in it. Not as a showcase of his wealth. It had lots of bedrooms and he'd ensured there was plenty of comfortable space.

The gray stone blended perfectly with the wooded acres the house was situated on. A good many mature trees surrounded it for climbing and tree houses.

He'd imagined the pitter-patter of little feet on the antique maple-wood floors. Thanksgiving dinner in the dining room, which overlooked the pond. He wasn't set up for kids yet, so his family rarely visited him here. It was easier to meet at their houses. But he would still dream about it. Just not like this…

So why did it feel so right when he took Ivy's hand and led her into the house and around the lower floor? He tried to tell himself the gesture was necessary in case she was tired or feeling sick. But the truth was that he had an overwhelming urge to touch her once more.

Especially in this moment. Inside his house.

Attempting to pull his mind away from their one night in this house and back to the consequences, Paxton led Ivy down a short hallway to the one downstairs bedroom. "I thought we'd put you in here."

It wasn't until he noticed her staring at the bed that Paxton realized what he'd done. He was thinking of her comfort…not the fact that this was the room where they'd spent the night together.

Bluff it out.

"I figured this would be more comfortable for you than having to climb the stairs to the other bedrooms."

"I'm not disabled, Paxton," she murmured.

He couldn't tell if her tone held hurt or pain or maybe even relief.

"I realize that," he conceded. "I just wanted to make things easier."

Where was that ready charm that usually came so easily to him? Normally he was in and out of an embarrassing moment quick as a wink. Today he felt as paralyzed and awkward as a schoolboy.

So he might as well get the other awkward conversation out of the way. "I also want you to know... you don't have to worry."

"About what?"

"I haven't told anyone you're here, per your request. Including my family."

He'd been surprised when she'd made that a condition of her decision to move in with him, but upon reflection he could understand. It was for the best, for now. The last thing this volatile situation needed was his grandmother's involvement. And her demand was easily accommodated, since his family didn't usually come to his house.

"Do you regret having me here already?"

The unexpected question pulled his gaze to her. Something in her still, small voice compelled him. But he couldn't see any condemnation in her eyes... just genuine concern. For him.

"No..." he said. "I should, but I don't."

As soon as the words were out, he regretted them. Honesty wasn't always the best policy. He didn't want to hurt her, but he was also leery of giving away too much. There were reasons he needed her at arm's length...in another room...on another floor. He needed to remember that.

"Besides, keeping quiet makes my life—with my family—a lot less complicated. As long as we both agree to keep it that way." Why he felt the need to add that caveat right at this moment, he wasn't sure. But he knew immediately he'd given too much away.

"Have I ever given you a reason not to trust me?" she asked, startling him.

He didn't like the idea that she could read what he was thinking. "No, of course not," he answered readily. "Well, until you disappeared without telling me."

"I told you I was leaving. I just didn't tell you where I was going. But I have a feeling that's not all that's going on here."

Paxton looked away. He wasn't sure he'd be able to keep the past where it belonged. Under lock and key. The last thing he wanted to talk to Ivy about was how gullible and vulnerable he'd been as a young man. He'd taken many steps to protect himself since then.

Lessons learned.

She went on, "Well, I think maybe we need to come up with a plan. Don't you?"

As if his body recognized the way out, his muscles relaxed. Now she was talking his language. Paxton grinned. At the office, he asked about "the plan" first thing every morning. Every meeting ended with a review of "the plan" going forward.

They'd certainly jumped into this situation without one. Maybe a more businesslike approach would get them both back on track.

"What is the purpose here?" she murmured. "We're in this for the long haul, I guess." She glanced at him before her eyes widened. "I mean, not this." She gestured to the bedroom before them. "But this." Her slim hand then motioned between the two of them. "Oh dear." Her cheeks were now beet red. "I mean—"

"It's okay," Paxton reassured her, though he couldn't hold in a smile. "I know what you mean. A goal would make it easier to know when we've arrived, right?"

Her glance flickered back toward the bed before she averted her gaze. "Definitely. And I think if we focus on getting to know each other, building a strong base so that when the baby comes, we can make decisions together."

He nodded. That's where the focus needed to be... not on the bed they'd spent the night in, or any bed at all. "No matter what, we'll be working together. This is just a different arena than it was before. This is personal, not professional."

Just not too personal.

"So, how are you feeling today?"

The awkward question was not at all how Ivy had imagined starting off dinner tonight. She'd hoped to serve something really nice to celebrate Paxton's first full day back at work and her ability to actually handle raw food without feeling sick. Instead they were sitting down to dinner two hours late to dried-out fettuccine Alfredo and grilled chicken that had gone from raw to the consistency of cardboard.

"Well, I was able to handle raw meat today," she said hesitantly, grabbing the first thing that came to mind.

"That's a plus." He seemed happy, but his smile was strained around the edges.

She hadn't cooked since right before she found out she was pregnant. The smells were simply more than her queasy stomach could handle. But she was fast approaching the threshold that the doctor had told her about, and with each day the nausea retreated. She was actually close to having true morning sickness, instead of all-day sickness.

Miracle of miracles.

"Your kitchen is incredible," she said, searching for a new topic of conversation.

When Paxton had finally come through the door, Ivy wasn't sure what to think. Instead of the easygoing boss she was used to seeing in the office, or the laid-back caretaker she'd dealt with over the last couple of weeks, Paxton seemed highly stressed and irritated at the moment. Even though he didn't show it much beyond his tightened mouth and overly bland expression, Ivy could somehow sense it in the vibrations coming off him.

But he seemed to relax a little more with the compliment. "It sure makes cooking a pleasure," he said with his trademark grin.

Ivy had marveled over the difference between their dated but charming kitchen at Auntie's and the miles of stainless-steel appliances and natural Italian tile in Paxton's.

She'd been afraid of messing something up, but quickly pushed the fear aside because she wanted to do something nice for Paxton. He'd been extremely attentive when he'd been home, and had waited to go back to work full-time for over a week. He hadn't had to do that, but she was more than grateful for the chance to get back on her feet.

Her family had been, too, when they'd returned from their trip. Ivy and Paxton had gone over there for a slightly awkward lunch, during which stories of her family's travels distracted them from thoughts that none of them said out loud... Too bad it was written in almost every expression. They'd been surprised to find Ivy staying with Paxton, and even more surprised when he mentioned packing some of her stuff. But other than a few quietly whispered questions to make sure she was okay, they hadn't meddled.

Which was kind of shocking, in and of itself.

Still, even after the intimacy they had shared at Auntie's, and upon their arrival here, Ivy couldn't handle tonight's unspoken conflict. The stiff, arm's-length business. As though they had regressed to strangers who had never worked together, never slept together. He'd been like this since yesterday. Maybe that's what she'd been trying to break through with this dinner.

Which was a complete disaster.

Paxton's phone dinged, and he rose to retrieve it from the bar countertop. He glanced at the screen, then sighed, running fingers through his blond hair as he stomped back to his chair. The careful mask slipped, and Ivy could more clearly see the frustration in his expression.

"Is everything okay?" she asked, unable to ignore his distress.

"What?" He glanced up as if just remembering she was there. "Oh, sure." He picked at his food again.

Well, this wasn't going according to plan. But then again, nothing in Ivy's life in the last three months had gone the way she'd wanted it to.

As she watched him shuffle his food around on his plate, Ivy remembered all of the wonderful meals he'd cooked for her. Guilt reared its ugly head. "I'm sorry," she blurted out.

Paxton froze, glancing around the table as if trying to find the source of her regret. "About what?"

"That dinner isn't very good." She shook her head. "I can cook, I promise. I just don't know how to fix it when it dries out."

Paxton shot her a sad grin. "After several hours, I don't think there's much you can do. Don't worry. I didn't bring you here to cook for me." He held her gaze, as if trying to convey a meaning he didn't know how to say out loud. "But, Ivy, I do appreciate the thought."

His weariness truly registered. The stress that had seemed to build under the surface the last few days was out in the open. And he was checking his phone during a meal when he would normally have left it until later. Maybe this wasn't really about her?

"Is work going okay?" She wasn't sure if it was her place to ask, since she wasn't his wife or his secretary, but she couldn't *not* ask.

He rubbed at his forehead. "Honestly, no." Another ping from his phone. She couldn't imagine who would be texting him from the office at this hour, unless there was a major incident. After-hours communication, outside of emergencies, wasn't a habit that Paxton had ever developed.

"Oh, for Christ's sake!" Paxton dropped his phone onto the table, then got up to pace.

Watching his trek back and forth increased her worry. She fiddled with her cloth napkin. What could've gone so wrong?

"Is there anything I can help with?" she asked.

He froze midstep. "Not unless you're willing to come back to work for me."

Her eyes widened, and she shifted back in her chair in surprise. Was he kidding? Or serious?

But before he could follow up, his phone rang. He swiped to connect the call, his expression tense. His lips were tight as he said, "Hello?"

His grip on the top of the kitchen chair grew tighter and tighter as the minutes passed, until Ivy could see the strain in his knuckles from across the table.

"Yes, Mrs. Holden. Yes, we probably need to get that straightened out."

Realizing that his new assistant might be the source of his irritation was actually a relief to Ivy, though she wouldn't be petty enough to admit it. She quickly retrieved the bottle of wine and refilled his glass while he finished the call. He gave lots of clipped responses before he signed off, none of them seeming to relate to an accident or emergency. Just some kind of mix-up. Then Paxton sank into his chair and took a large swallow of wine before letting his gaze meet hers.

"This is not going to work," he said.

"But she did so well when I was training her," Ivy said. "What went wrong?"

"It's the scheduling. She's great with most of the paperwork and greeting people and all of that stuff, but she can't keep my calendar for anything. And I end up with texts like this—" he lifted his cell phone so she could see the displayed lists of texts from tonight "—at the end of the day because things didn't appear in my calendar. And even though I now know it's for tomorrow, I can't plan at the last minute. Everything I've already put in place for the next day has to be rearranged. It's just a mess."

Knowing how important it was to Paxton that he be in places on time and prepared, and add to that the set amount of hours he dedicated to working in the office every day, told her just how annoying this would be to him.

"I feel like I should fix this," she said.

"Why?" he asked, cocking his head to the side. "It's not your fault."

"Well, I am the one who helped put her in that position. I even gave a recommendation to HR."

Paxton studied Ivy from across the length of the table. It wasn't huge, but it wasn't small either; there was just enough distance between them that she couldn't read his expression in detail. Mostly she saw curiosity. Concern.

"I'm serious," he said.

She swallowed hard, feeling like some of the dried pasta was stuck in her throat. "About what?"

"Would you consider coming back to work for me?"

Ivy was surprised by how much she wanted to do just that. During her time as his assistant, she had excelled. She felt far from excellent at the moment.

But she shook her head. "I don't think that's a good idea. Someone could find out…" Not to mention her own personal pull toward her boss. Though she didn't want to talk about sexual attraction with him, she knew for a fact it was alive and kicking… for her, at least.

"We don't have to advertise anything at the office," he said, enthusiasm growing in his expression. "I promise not to make any casual personal comments. Heck, I would even be happy with you working from home. Part-time. Full-time. I'll take whatever you want to give me."

He couldn't know how good those words sounded. If only he meant them in a different way.

"But as things become more obvious," she said with a gesture toward her still flat tummy, "what will you tell people?"

He shrugged, a desperate light in his eyes. "For now, it's the perfect excuse for you quitting, then coming back full time. No one would guess who the father was." He glanced away, as if realizing how dismissive that might sound. After a moment, he looked back. "I realize this is selfish of me to ask. But I promise, we will work out the details. You know my family…they aren't the most observant of—"

"The help?" She supplied the word for him, only letting a little of her judgment seep into her tone.

He grinned. "Yeah. I'm not saying it's right. It's just who they are. Even if they notice your pregnancy, they wouldn't be interested enough to ask."

Ivy knew that was the truth, from her own experience of them. But that didn't keep her unease at bay. Just to clarify, she asked, "Is she really that bad?"

"Not really. But I just…I like how we worked together. You ran my office smoothly. I had absolutely no complaints. And I just want that back."

Ivy never thought she'd be so tempted by a job offer. But was it really wise? Were there complications besides the obvious that she was missing?

"I know I'm putting you in an awkward position," Paxton said. "And I don't mean to. But desperate times…" He shook his phone at her. "Please, Ivy. We worked so well together. Let's just try it. There's plenty of time to figure the rest out. We'll tackle that when it becomes an issue."

Again, the best laid plans…

There were probably some parameters she should put into place, but her brain wouldn't comprehend what they were at this moment. She simply knew that she herself would love to return to the rhythm of her days from before that fateful night three months ago. She couldn't resist. But would she find later that she'd made a deal with the devil?

Nine

This was not going according to Paxton's perfect plan.

He watched from the doorway as Ivy handled a phone call at the desk that she had occupied for so long before her pregnancy. Simultaneously she input information into his schedule with smooth key strokes. After a few moments, he felt the vibration of his phone in his pocket as he was automatically notified of the change.

It sure was good to see her there. But not in the way that he had expected. She was great at her job, but he was seeing so much more that he hadn't when they had worked together before—the small curling tendrils that brushed her neck when her hair was up, the electricity that accompanied every accidental touch or the way she nibbled at her lips when she was concentrating.

Why had he never noticed how red and kissable that made her mouth?

Her poise, her ability to defuse potential problems, even how she handled things with a calm facade when he could tell she wasn't really feeling well remained the same.

But she seemed to be better lately. The morning commute was a little iffy, and occasionally he would notice her slipping one of the little ginger lozenges into her mouth during the day. She was only working part-time...three quarters of the time when she felt up to it, but it was enough for him to start relying on her again.

He was grateful that she was doing so well, but they hadn't addressed the baby lately. Maybe tonight, though. He needed to ask about her next doctor's appointment. Even though they'd returned to being boss and assistant, he wanted her to remember that he was first and foremost there for her and the baby.

Things between them had changed more than he'd wanted to admit. Before he'd seen her exclusively as an employee. Well...maybe not. He'd tried. He'd known there had been an attraction there, but they'd both steadfastly avoided it.

Somehow the knowledge that his assistant was pregnant with his baby added a feeling of intimacy to their time here together, no matter how focused they were on business. He was grateful that she was so good at her job, but the atmosphere between them was completely different. He liked that.

More than he wanted to admit.

Watching her hands, her mouth, reminded him of that night together so long ago. It seemed like forever since he'd touched her. But he wished that he could touch her again. More than just the briefest of brushes that he experienced here. Even more than the intimacy of washing her hair in the bathtub.

He even found himself wondering if there was a way he could make it work outside of the office. For real.

The temptation grew with every day they were together. He knew he should run away fast. But he simply couldn't. Neither his feeling of obligation as the baby's father nor the fact that he actually cared what happened to Ivy, and that she not feel her life had been waylaid, would let him get too far away.

The phone in his pocket buzzed again, this time announcing that he had a phone call. Which meant it was family…

With a last long look at Ivy, he turned back into his office. Then he swiped to answer the call from his mother.

"Hello," he greeted her simply, wondering why she would call him during the day on his cell.

She didn't make him wait for long.

"Well, if it isn't my long-lost son," she said, sarcasm heavy in her words. "I was beginning to wonder if you would answer the phone if I called."

Paxton felt the unexpected urge to snap at her, but

reined himself in. "What can I do for you, Mother?" His tight control couldn't stop the formality from creeping into his voice.

"For starters you could tell me if you're coming to Sunday dinner. Or are you going to skip again this week…with no excuse?"

"I have every intention of being there," Paxton assured her.

And he did. Things had been kind of hectic until he had gotten Ivy settled in. But he'd kept his promise, and hadn't mentioned her to his family. They had too much to decide first.

Still he couldn't keep ignoring them. So Sunday dinner was the minimum he could do.

"See that you are," she said. "Otherwise we might start to think that you have a secret that you're hiding from us."

The muscles along Paxton's back tensed up, creating an ache at the base of his skull. That was the last thing he needed them thinking.

"I don't know why you would think that, Mother," he said, anxious to deflect her attention from anything that might lead to snooping. "You know things have been hectic since I was out of town for so long. It's just taking a lot to get back on track."

"And that's why I've tried not to bug you," she said. "But I can only put this on hold for so long."

"Put what on hold?"

"Why, dinner with the Baxters." Her tone indicated she expected praise for this announcement.

Paxton frowned. The name sounded vaguely familiar. "I'm not sure I follow." Socializing was a regular requirement for both their business progress and social standing, but what was so important about this particular family?

"I can't believe you don't remember me mentioning this before you left. Where is your brain, Paxton? I would think you of all people would be excited."

"About what?" He glanced out the window of his office to see Ivy studying a file. Guilt and need mingled inside his gut. He wished his mother would just spit it out. But sometimes she truly enjoyed stringing the conversation along. It made her feel more in control.

"I told you that the Baxters' daughter has moved home. She was off at one of those fancy colleges, getting another degree, and now she's back here, interviewing for jobs. Not that she would need to work if she got herself a successful wealthy, business-minded husband. Goodness knows all that learning is a bit much."

Oh man. He could not handle matchmaking right now. It was the last thing he needed. "Mom, I'm not sure—"

"She would be perfect for you. Pretty, poised and able to handle the circles that you socialize with, network with. Obviously she's smart, so she should have plenty to talk about. You should at least give it one dinner." Her tone brooked no argument.

Thankfully she wasn't there to see him roll his eyes. How could he admit to his mother that the last thing he wanted was another woman in his life right now? He had enough going on at the moment, and he had enough conflicts over this thing with Ivy to keep his psyche occupied for quite a while.

"We can talk about it later, Mother."

"We can talk about it at Sunday dinner. I even have pictures."

At least Paxton got his stubbornness honestly. He and his mom had clashed throughout the years, but he still loved her. She reminded him of his grandmother in force of personality, even though she was a daughter-in-law, and she'd be a solid leader for their family once his grandmother was gone. He loved her, but sometimes her desire to lead her children where she wanted them to go was more than a little heavy-handed.

But after he rang off, Paxton felt guilt settle into his gut. His family had always come first in his life, business second. They were often intertwined. He hated lying to his family, even when he knew his mother was trying to manipulate him.

He should be thrilled that his mother wanted to introduce him to a woman who fit into the plan *he'd* talked about for so long. A wife raised in his own social circles, able to understand the subtleties of high-society conversations and interactions, a woman able to step into high-pressure situations with poise and ease. A woman who already knew many of the people he dealt with on Savannah's social landscape.

As his office door opened and Ivy came through, Paxton felt that conflict build. Ivy could do many of those things with a little training, but he couldn't change the circumstances of her birth, her upbringing. He might want to overlook her station, explain away her occupation by saying that she would soon have a high-profile brother-in-law. But he knew the truth.

His family would never accept her...and neither would she fit into the plan he'd laid out for his life.

His thoughts were interrupted by the big smile she offered him as she reached his desk. "Thank you," she said.

Her comment caught him off guard. "For what?"

"For giving me this chance. It's so good to be back. Thank you for overlooking the issues..." She gestured between them. "I'd been trying to find another job, but deep down I knew that I really enjoyed working here and I missed it."

"I didn't know you'd been looking for work."

"Well, I was, between bouts of morning sickness." She shot him a rueful grin. "I've always had a big need to support myself. You know, it's one of those control things."

They shared a glance full of knowledge.

"Anyway," she went on, "I know it will be complicated later. But I do love my job. I think I'm damn good at my job. I just wanted you to know that this means a lot to me."

In a rush, Ivy put her arms around him for an all-too-brief moment, then hurried back to her desk.

Paxton wanted to follow her. Her happiness and enthusiasm drew him. She was passionate about her work, and he could have all that passion directed toward him—he remembered that experience all too well. All he had to do was give up his perfect plans for his future.

And his family's support.

"You seem awfully calm for a man about to baby-sit a toddler," Ivy said as Paxton drove them to Jasmine and Royce's place near the historic district of Savannah.

"I have plenty of experience," he said, utter confidence in his words and body.

It was the same confidence with which he drove his luxury sports car, which still had that new-car smell despite being several years old. Paxton's grip on the steering wheel was loose and easy.

Ivy wished she felt the same. She loved her niece and had always enjoyed spending time with her... before. Now between the thankfully still-rare toddler tantrums and her own impending motherhood, Ivy was beginning to wonder if she was cut out for the day in, day out stresses of being a mother. It just all seemed so complicated, with every little decision fraught with the potential to scar her child for life. Something she became more aware of with each passing day.

How in the world had she gotten signed up for that?

They rode the elevator to the top floor of Royce's building in silence, with Ivy still feeling jealous of Paxton's quiet confidence. She tried not to show her nerves as Jasmine let them in, holding a little girl with dark curly hair who had a cherubic smile that could turn to tears at the least sign of resistance.

Sure enough, her birthday was right around the corner, and she'd be two.

"Thank you so much," her sister rushed to say. "With Auntie sick and Willow restricted from lifting anything, I was in a panic about tonight."

"Not a problem," Paxton said.

Jasmine sent him a questioning look, but didn't say anything as Royce made an appearance. They looked like the perfect high-society couple—Royce in his black tux, Jasmine in a sparkling floor-length gown and heels.

Ivy felt grubby beside them in her jeans and T-shirt, even though she knew it was the most practical choice for playing with a toddler.

Rosie came straight to Ivy when she held out her arms to the little girl, settling comfortably against her while eyeing the stranger in her house with suspicion. Rosie was more used to being around girls than guys, and it definitely showed. Jasmine pulled them both into a hug as Royce shook Paxton's hand.

"I'm so glad you're feeling better," she whispered against Ivy's ear.

Then off they went, glamour personified. The opposite of all the nights Ivy hung out at home in her sweats these days.

Not that she was jealous or anything. She settled the toddler onto her feet. "Rosie, let's show Paxton your toys."

She led him into the gorgeous main room of the suite, which constituted half the floor of the renovated building. Royce still had the brown suede furniture from when this had been his bachelor pad. A large flat-screen television and entertainment center sat in one corner. Several oversize rugs were strategically placed to help soften the polished plank floor for Rosie's tender feet, and one corner now held a play kitchen and shelves of toys for her. Toys and children's DVDs were something Ivy would never have imagined seeing in this room the first time she'd walked into it.

But the main attraction and focus of the room was still the glass walls that looked out over the city of Savannah. It was absolutely gorgeous, especially on a night like this, when soft lights decorated the dark panoramic view.

The view gave the room an air of sophistication despite the new family-style touches.

Paxton was obviously impressed, but quickly turned his attention back to Rosie and her toys.

"Whatcha got, pretty girl?"

In the way that only children can, Rosie went from giving Paxton the side-eye to being his best buddy in record time. Ivy found herself relegated to helper status throughout dinner and Rosie's bath, but it was Rosie's insistence that Paxton alone put her to bed that was the kicker for her fragile self-image.

Left alone, Ivy stared out the window as she waited in the living area, worries whirling around in her brain. Without thinking, she crossed her arms tightly over her stomach, as if hugging her body to comfort herself. Maybe the stance would hold in all the stupid emotions that kept washing over her, but Ivy couldn't hold back the few tears that slipped down her cheeks. Disgusted, she wiped her face to erase the evidence of her weakness.

"Are you okay?"

Ivy jumped. Of course Paxton would come back into the room at right that moment, instead of granting her the dignity to hide her emotional response to something that shouldn't affect her at all. She mumbled about stupid hormones to brush it off as easily as the tears from her cheeks.

"They are the bane of a woman's existence, from what I've been told," Paxton joked.

Ivy couldn't help giving a tired laugh. "You smooth talker, you."

She watched his approach in the reflection from the windows until he walked into the shadows directly behind her.

"I do my best," he said. "But I wouldn't mind knowing what's going on with you. You've been awfully quiet tonight."

"I've been replaced, apparently," she said, then instantly felt embarrassed by the confession. Her niece was just a toddler, after all.

Paxton moved in close, as if he wanted to hug her but was afraid to… Would he reject her if she leaned back against his chest? Would he welcome that kind of intimacy these days? Or would he turn away from her, embarrassed that she'd presumed too much?

"Toddlers are fickle creatures," Paxton said.

Ivy tightened her arms around her torso. If no one else would hug her, that's the only comfort she had.

She knew her fears were unfounded, but still… "What if I'm not a good mother?" she mumbled.

Paxton was silent for a moment, as if he hadn't heard her clearly, then he asked, "Why would you think that?"

More than anything, Ivy wanted to pace back and forth before the windows, to expend the energy driving her emotions, but she also didn't want to face Paxton. Or move away from him. Instead the energy went into tapping her foot against the plank floor.

Her stomach cramped, but it wasn't nausea this time. It was stupid nerves. "I'm not one of those women who has spent a lifetime dreaming of marriage and family."

At least, not the family part. All of Ivy's daydreams had focused on the romance leading up to the happily ever after. She shrugged. "What if I'm just not good at it? The chores I can handle. But what if I do something really stupid and screw him or her up?"

Paxton chuckled, finally moving in close and wrapping his arms around her this time. She went still with shock, her foot going quiet. He was heated comfort, with that edge of sizzle.

"Don't worry," Paxton said. "I have plenty of money for therapy if they need it."

Ivy jolted. *They?*

Paxton squeezed a little tighter, bringing the front of his body into delicious alignment with her back. It should've been a platonic move, but it wasn't. Not for Ivy.

"You know what?" he asked.

"What?"

He rested his cheek against her hair. A gesture that made her heart ache. "We made a baby together," he said softly, his reverent tone surprising her. "How awesome is that?"

"I've been so focused on keeping food down and not being terrified that I forget sometimes," she said in a hushed voice that matched his. "Is that terrible?"

"No, it's coping the best you can. That's all any of us can do, Ivy," he reassured her. "Trust me—if you didn't care enough about the baby, you wouldn't question whether you'd be a good mother or not."

"I don't want to screw this up. For the baby, for me...for you."

"You won't. Besides, I'll be there to help."

"So this baby can love you more, too?" Ivy realized she was only half joking. Paxton had lived up to his words, playing hands-on daddy all night to a kid who had loved, loved, loved it.

Could she really live up to someone like that?

"Oh, I doubt my child will find me as much of a novelty."

The only reason she could think of for that was if he was rarely there. How hard would it be to watch Paxton only visit on the weekends? Would his commitment to his child wain? Would he get tired of trying to share and decide to go for full custody?

"I hope not," she murmured.

Ten

"Hey, Willow. How's life on the island?"

Ivy fiddled with the cord of the phone on her desk as she answered the call from her sister.

Willow had moved to one of the outer islands off Savannah's coast to be with her significant other. Tate had been one of the biggest secrets in Savannah, and still lived the life of a semi-reclusive author. But being involved with one of the Harden sisters had given him a much-needed social life. He was a man who had interesting ties to their family history—just as they had ties to his future. Willow was currently pregnant with his twins.

"I've got a surprise," Willow said.

By her excited tone, it must be a really good surprise. Of course Ivy had always known bookworm

Willow to get excited about the strangest things. "Well, spit it out!"

Willow chuckled before launching into her subject. "So, the ledger we found in Sabatini House's attic, the one from Tate's ancestors that had the contracts in it for all of his illicit business, well…" She paused for dramatic effect, a tactic Ivy was more than familiar with Willow using. "Tate found the man's family. The one who was contracted for the night the McLemores' ship went down."

One of Willow's deciding factors in going to Sabatini House to work for Tate as a housekeeper had been to find evidence that their family was not responsible for sinking the McLemores' ship. She had found a ledger in a dusty room on the abandoned third floor with contracts between Tate's great-grandfather and various disreputable men in Savannah. There was a contract for the night in question, with not nearly enough details. What they really needed to know now was what it meant.

Could they use it to create reasonable doubt of their family's involvement? Or even to prove their innocence?

"Really? Is it a family that still lives around here?"

"Only a couple of hours away. We're going up there on Thursday, just to see what they can tell us."

Ivy wasn't so sure about this plan. "Do you think they'll actually appreciate you accusing their ancestor of sinking a ship? Murdering people?"

"Don't you know this is the South? We don't hide

our crazy people in the attic. We bring them right out onto the front porch."

Having heard the expression before, Ivy smiled. It faded fast as she realized once more where she was... and what they were discussing.

"But the man was a murderer," Ivy reminded her, lowering her voice as she glanced toward Paxton's office.

"Some families enjoy talking about their notorious relatives," Willow reminded her, not concerned in the least. "We will see when we get there... For someone who has avoided people so much, Tate has done a lot of interviews for his books. He says it will be fine. Trust him."

"I'm trying," Ivy said, squeezing her eyes shut. While she wanted to trust that the future was going to work itself out, she was having more than a little trouble with her faith at the moment.

"This could be the evidence we need to prove Tate's family hired the person who sank that ship. How do you think Paxton would feel if we could prove our family was actually innocent?"

Ivy shook her head. "I honestly don't know." She'd never considered the fact that her family was thought to have damaged his when contemplating her feelings for him. Mostly because she'd never thought those feelings would be returned. On the night they'd been together, her family history had been the last thing on her mind.

Would he embrace her if she confessed, with the evidence that it wasn't really an issue? Or would there be other things that stood in the way? Who was she kidding? Of course there were other issues, some she could only guess at, since Paxton had retreated from her way before he knew the truth of who she was. She had no idea how he would feel when he found out how notorious her family really was.

Ivy murmured, "I don't know."

But she desperately needed this back-up plan, because the truth would come out eventually, and she needed to mitigate the damage as much as possible. Parenting would be awkward enough without his relatives shunning her child over something her family had not been involved in.

"How exciting will it be to know what really happened?" Willow enthused, her love of history and family fusing into one explosive firework over this subject. "I can't wait!"

Ivy chuckled. "You're such a nerd."

"You know it."

"Thank you, Willow. And thank Tate for me, too. I don't know what I'd do without all of your help."

Ivy ran off before she could get too emotional. She took a deep breath, trying to regain her equilibrium. "Everything will be okay," she murmured under her breath, then got out of her chair. Only to find Paxton watching her from his doorway.

She shot a panicked glance at the phone. How much had he heard?

"Everything all right?" he asked.

She pasted on a bright, forced smile. "Isn't that my line?"

His shrewd gaze narrowed; he wasn't buying the brush-off as quickly as she'd have liked.

"Is something wrong?" He glanced down at the hand she'd unknowingly rested on her still-flat tummy. "Everything okay with the baby?"

The genuine concern in his amber eyes was almost more than Ivy could handle. She raised a hand as if swearing on a Bible. Though it was a good thing she wasn't. All the secrets she was keeping would surely send her to hell in a handbasket.

"Absolutely nothing. I was just talking to Willow about a new plot of Tate's. You know, supersecret author stuff."

The look in Paxton's eyes slowly morphed from concerned to questioning. *I'm not very good at secrets.* He advanced on her carefully, step-by-step from across the room. Each move made her heart pound.

How could a simple walk be sexy enough for her body to react?

"Are you lying?" he asked, drawing out each word.

Nerves caused her throat to close up, refusing to let out the words. She shook her head. She couldn't let Paxton find out about her family. Not yet. The fallout wasn't something she was ready to face.

"I think you are." His voice deepened, taking on a sexy, teasing tone that she'd thought she'd never hear again. "What do I need to do to get to the truth?"

He couldn't ever know the truth. Then again, if he kept walking like that, she might break her resolve in a heartbeat.

Paxton's eyes widened as he reached the halfway point, awareness suddenly flaring in his eyes. Awareness of the game he was playing. Danger seemed to shimmer between them. Ivy knew she shouldn't mess with the undercurrents she felt, but this game wasn't in her hands anymore.

Paxton kept moving forward, holding her gaze, until he came close enough to bury his hands in her hair.

His husky voice sent shivers over her body as he asked, "Are you sure there's nothing you want to tell me?"

"What's going on in here?"

For a moment Paxton thought he'd only imagined his sister's voice—a figment of his guilty imagination. But no. One glance to the side showed Alicia staring wide-eyed at him from just inside the door to his office suite.

Caught with his hands in the cookie jar...

Sierra would have been far preferable, as she was the more forgiving, tactful sibling. He jerked back, only to have Ivy cry out and press a palm to her scalp.

"I'm sorry, Ivy," he murmured, but there was no time to lose in diverting Alicia's attention. He turned fully toward his sister in order to block her view of Ivy.

"Alicia, what brings you here?" he asked, forcing himself to appear calm and collected, when inside his body was instantly primed and ready for a fight.

Actually, he realized it was primed and ready to

protect Ivy. Which was not how he would have imagined this same scenario six months ago. Then everything would have truly been calm and collected. Actually, this entire scenario would never have happened.

His sister raised her blond brow, a typical expression of hers that matched her slightly acerbic personality. "Apparently I'm not coming in often enough," she said.

In an attempt to derail her from having this conversation in front of Ivy, Paxton crossed to his sister and marched her to his inner office with a hand on her arm.

"What I do in my office isn't any of your business," he stated under his breath, hoping to spare Ivy any embarrassment.

His sister didn't share his qualms. She used what his mother would have called her "outside voice" to say, "Since Grandmother still controls the board of this company, I think she'd be very interested in what happens in this office."

Paxton shuffled her inside the inner sanctum and closed the door with a little more force than necessary. Alicia had always been the more difficult sibling. They had butted heads many times over the years, though he would say that overall their relationship was a good one.

"Don't start with me," he warned.

She adopted a *who me?* expression. "I'm just trying to figure out if this is the 'work' that's been keeping you so occupied."

"Let it go," he growled.

Alicia wandered around the room, trailing her fingers over his bookshelf. "Why?" She tossed him a mischievous glance over her shoulder. The kind that had always spelled trouble for him when they were teenagers. "Torturing you is so much fun."

"This isn't a game, Alicia."

Certainly not one he wanted to play. If his grandmother got wind of any involvement with his assistant, it would go very badly for Ivy. Not that Paxton couldn't protect her, but his grandmother would make her life miserable in the meantime.

"I think it might be, especially since Mother is trying to set you up with that Baxter chick."

How did that get around? Paxton settled into his chair with a creak of leather and a sigh. "Nice to know my, um, professional life is so interesting to everyone."

"Your recent absence—and how unusual that is— has made you a very common topic...just among family, though."

That's reassuring. Paxton leaned back to stare at the ceiling. "Ah, the joys of a close-knit family."

His sister crossed over to rest her hip against his desk. "Any information you'd like to grant me permission to share would definitely up my credibility with the old lady."

"Well, this—" he waved his hand toward the window, where they could see Ivy working at her desk "—is not something anyone needs to worry about. A complete nonissue. Now—" he gave her a stern look "—what did you come by for?"

In an unusual move, Alicia turned her attention down to her impeccable manicure. "I just wondered if you had noticed anything off with Sierra?"

Paxton thought back over the cryptic words Sierra had spoken to him at the doctor's office and how often her husband had been absent lately. Paxton may not have been very involved with family matters since returning from his trip, but that was one thing he'd kept on the edge of his awareness.

"Not really," he hedged, not wanting to give a hint of what he suspected in case it caused problems for Sierra. "Why?"

"She's just been pretty emotional lately."

"She is pregnant," he reminded her. Alicia should know all about those strange pregnancy mood swings after two children of her own.

"Even so... I'd hate for her to do anything rash based solely on pregnancy hormones."

Paxton leaned forward, training his gaze on his sister and her unusually meandering conversation. Normally she was much more direct than this. "Because you think she might..."

Finally Alicia met his gaze. "She's made quite a few remarks about her husband being absent. How he lost interest in them once he knew this baby was also a girl. How when he is home, he's always locked up in his study. That kind of thing."

Now, that was news to Paxton. But then he thought back to what she'd said that day at the hospital. *Just because the whole business-before-pleasure thing worked for our parents and grandparents doesn't mean it's the wonderful life they told us it would be. Marrying for money is just as complicated as marrying for love.*

"If that's true, it sounds like she's got good reason to be unhappy," he mused, upset he was just now paying true attention to the signs.

"Feelings should not be a reason to make major changes," Alicia insisted. "Especially with her husband this close to sitting on the board." She held her fingers up an inch apart.

Better now than later. Though he didn't say it, Paxton had the uncomfortable urge to defend his sister's right to make decisions based on how she felt. He settled for saying, "No matter how logical it seems for the business—and Jason has done a great job in his position—that doesn't mean she has to be miserable for the rest of her life." He stood up, feeling the need to brace himself. "That's what the prenup is for."

"You're not helping, Paxton." Obviously that wasn't what she wanted to hear.

But he couldn't stop the thoughts from crowding in—thoughts contrary to everything he'd been taught his whole life. "Maybe it's time we started worrying about our sister more than we do the bottom line."

He stomped out his agitation as he walked to the door. He was more than ready for this conversation to be over. Luckily his sister went with him. He wasn't prepared for her to go back to the earlier subject, though.

"Is ignoring the bottom line going to protect you with the hired help?" she asked, nodding her head toward Ivy. "You know, when she gets herself pregnant and all."

Alicia probably thought she was being funny, but Paxton felt a flare of anger that loosened his tongue, just as it had when they were teens.

"I won't need a prenup," he said, frustration over his current situation and how his family would view it prodding him hard. "I'm smart enough to know my assistant isn't marriage material."

Only when he caught Alicia's smirk did he realize she had opened the office door before he spoke those infamous last words.

Eleven

Ivy could tell from Paxton's body language that he was upset and quickly putting up his emotional guard. Only, she couldn't tell if it was to continue the confrontation with his sister, or because he'd been caught red-handed by Ivy. Of course, he could probably read the same emotions in her body, too…if he was paying any attention at all.

His sister left without a word. That was Alicia's usual exit when Paxton wasn't around, but it was even more pointed today, given what had transpired. He didn't watch her go. Instead he stood right outside the door to his office, those watchful eyes cataloging Ivy's every move.

She knew exactly what emotions she was telegraphing. Big. Time. Anger. *Not marriage material.*

Humiliation burned like lava slowly spreading over her nerves. To have Paxton talk about her that way with his sister dug deep into Ivy's insecurities. Having him reduce her to her job, her station in life, left her ready to explode, but she deliberately locked those emotions down tightly.

She'd suspected that his family viewed her as less than from the first, but not Paxton. Never Paxton.

Silence settled after the door closed behind Alicia. Ivy didn't rush to fill it. She wanted to choose her words carefully, but the emotions churning inside of her muddled the connection between her brain and her mouth.

Finally she just opened her lips and let loose. "So, I'm good enough to knock up, but not good enough to marry?"

She hated the way her voice shook, but this was a conversation she wasn't walking away from. Not if they were to have any future relationship at all, even just one that consisted of co-parenting.

In contrast, his voice was even as he said, "I would never describe you like that."

"Why not?" She paused to swallow hard, desperately trying to keep her voice a few steps down from a yell. "Even if Alicia doesn't know the whole story, we both know it's what you meant. Assistants are not marriageable material, right? I should have known that's what the disappearing act was about..."

Paxton gave a single sharp shake of his head. "No, Ivy." As if he couldn't resist, he braced his body in his typical boardroom stance—legs locked, arms crossed over his chest. "Look, I'm sorry. I was trying to extricate myself from an uncomfortable conversation by saying what my sister would expect to hear."

Ivy wasn't buying it. "Apology not accepted. Why would you talk about me with her in the first place?"

Paxton took a step closer, his movement tentative, as if too much pressure would make her go off like a bomb. "We are very close. There was no way she wouldn't ask about what she walked in on."

That earlier near miss wasn't something Ivy wanted to talk about. Not right now.

"Which you explain away by bad-mouthing me?" she asked instead. "What a gentleman you are."

"My family—" he ran his hands through his hair "—they don't see things the way most people do."

"You're right. I have plenty of experience with them, right here in this office. They see people as objects—in terms of what purpose they can serve. Not who they really are."

He shook his head as if to deny it, but she wasn't letting him off the hook with this.

"I thought you were different, Paxton. Is that really how you want to live? Giving credence to that type of thinking?"

She stepped closer, her brain working through all the implications. Horror filling her as she thought about the future. "What about our child? I don't want him to think that's okay. That I'm inferior because I was Daddy's assistant."

Paxton took a deep breath. "You know I see you as more than that."

"They don't. Do you honestly think I'd let my child be alone with them so they can bad-mouth me when I'm not there?" Though how she'd prevent that, she wasn't sure.

"I would not let that happen."

"I want to believe you, but somehow you always end up disappointing me."

"What?" Surprise opened up his face, but she wasn't sure if it was because of her opinion or because she had the audacity to say it out loud.

It was that surprise that did her in—unlocking the churning emotions deep inside of her.

"Yes, Paxton. I spent the night with you, gave you my body, and you walked out without a word. I try to make decisions on my own, trying not to bother you until necessary, and I get accused of keeping secrets.

"I finally believe we are building some kind of partnership—" she almost choked on the word "—to raise our child, and I overhear you belittling me to your sister. I guess I'm the lesser partner in this arrangement." Ivy struggled not to let tears make an appearance, but she was failing.

"I've worked here for almost two years. You're a great boss and I appreciated that enough to keep my distance. I never thought it would happen, but then we moved beyond business. And it was the most incredible thing I've ever experienced." A white-hot wave of emotion washed over Ivy, blurring her vision with a flood of tears.

"I should have known the magic wasn't real. You were too good to be true, and I'm left trying to find the good in this nightmare. Is it just something about me? Something that won't let me have anything good that's truly mine?"

Ivy doubled over, the only way she knew to hide the tears that fell. It took a moment for the haze of anger and pain to dissipate, leaving her head clearer.

Actually too clear.

Ivy knew immediately she'd said something she shouldn't have. The last thing she'd wanted Paxton to know was how much their night together had meant to her, how deeply his disappearing act had hit her.

As she straightened, she could tell by the shell-shocked expression on his face that he'd gotten that message loud and clear. It hurt, because that expression meant she'd done a better job of hiding her feelings since he'd been home than she'd thought...or that he was completely clueless as to how she'd felt when they'd been together.

Then his expression darkened, intensifying as he studied her. But his look was far from analytical. More like a deep, hidden realization coming to life.

It became even more focused as he approached her. Her heartbeat picked up speed, causing her to catch her breath. Was he angry? Was he panicked? Was he—

Then his hands were in her hair once more and his lips covered hers. Ivy's world went dark and she gave herself over to the ultimate rush. There wasn't a single ounce of resistance in her body. At least not until he pulled back.

"I wasn't trying to put you down, Ivy. I was trying to throw Alicia off the trail. To protect you and our child from my family.

"It's sad that I had to do that, but I in no way meant to hurt you. The things you've said…these feelings you have…they're a more precious gift than anything I've ever been given. Never, ever forget that."

Ivy was lost in the whirlwind as Paxton locked them in his office and closed the blinds. With no guarantees, no resolution, she should not trust him, trust this… But something deep inside would not let her deny herself the chance for one more taste.

Each step he took toward her brought out a pulse of awareness that she didn't want to face. They were in his office—the ultimate no-touch zone. A combination of guilt and excitement mingled inside of her.

But when he moved in close, cupping her face as if her revelations had opened his eyes to her true self, she melted. Her shoulders relaxed as she dropped her guard. Her head fell back, granting him access to her vulnerable neck. The move was instinctive, a surrender to both his will and the emotions that had brought her here.

He lifted her to the credenza against the wall, crowding close between her legs. Though her skirt still covered her, its flowing style left her feeling exposed. His commanding presence overwhelmed the lingering fears in the back of her mind. As she braced herself with her arms behind her, Paxton took full advantage of her position to press even closer.

She tightened her thighs, unconsciously embracing

his hips, drawing him into her with her lower body. Fear held her back. Even though she ached to hold him close, Ivy could not get her arms to make the move. No matter how desperately she wanted him.

Then Paxton leaned in, resting his lips against the frantic pulse at the base of her throat. His mouth, his breath, were heated softness stroking her skin. He didn't rush or push for more. Instead he breathed deeply, inhaling her scent. A flash of heat shot through her, settling with a soft explosion between her thighs. Her soft cry echoed around them, a sound this room should never have heard.

Only then did Paxton open his mouth and cover the delicate spot. The sensations overwhelmed her. Soft, wet suction. The rumble of a groan deep in his throat. The tight grasp of his hands anchoring her on each side of her waist.

After long, heady minutes of his exquisite attention left her hot and edgy, he pulled back. His knuckles brushed the underside of her breast as he lifted his fingers to the two buttons of her suit jacket. He didn't move to open them, but instead held still.

Waiting. Then watching.

His head lifted. That intense amber gaze found hers and locked on. Mesmerized, she could not look away.

His fingers tightened as if it were all he could do not to rip the jacket open. Instead he asked, "Ivy?"

The questioning tone echoed in his expression. A need to acknowledge her permission; a desperation for it to be granted.

She wished she could ignore it, but the ache in his request hit her with a fierceness she hadn't expected, amplifying her own desires. She'd already laid herself bare. There was no denying him or herself right now.

So she answered simply, "Yes, Paxton," knowing there would be regret and pain further down the line. But his emotions and her own were a dynamic duo she couldn't walk away from.

It was short work for him to open her jacket, then the delicate blouse beneath. Her fuller breasts swelled over the cups of her bra, plump from the life growing inside of her. He brushed the creamy tops with his thumbs, followed by desperate sucking kisses. His attention to her breasts drew her deep into this moment, melting away any lingering fears for the future.

"Paxton," she murmured, wishing she had the courage to cradle his head in her hands.

Finally his palms pressed beneath the hem of her skirt, then squeezed the quivering muscles of her thighs. She felt a muffled curse against her breast as his fingers found the top edge of her thigh-high stockings, then another as they reached the damp material of her panties.

Ivy found herself slipping into a world of sounds and sensations as he worked his fingers around the barrier to explore her most intimate flesh.

Around and over and under until she wanted to weep in time with the pounding in her core. Then his teasing fingertips barely slipped inside of her. She couldn't stop the jerk of her hips, her body's attempt to draw him deeper. He eased in an inch more. Two fingers, then three.

At the same time, his whole body crowded closer. She found herself caught in his gaze once more, telling him things with her expression and movements that she would probably wish she had left hidden later on.

When sanity returned.

He worked her expertly, as if he knew just how to bring her greatest fears and fantasies to life. She tried not to think about the last time they'd done this—pure, exquisite pleasure, followed by so much pain.

"Paxton, please," she cried, her body skating the edge of ecstasy without the key that would push her past the brink.

"I need you," he said, pulling back to fumble with his pants. "Heaven help me, but I need you, Ivy."

In a matter of seconds, he had freed himself, bared her and was pressing against her lower lips. Ivy tilted her hips, granting him access. Her core seemed to suck him inside, so great was her need.

Only then did she allow her arms to embrace him, her hands to anchor him to her. He filled her to overflowing. Her every nerve jumped straight to overload. Her entire world narrowed to the feel of him moving inside of her, the sound of his desperate draws of air, and the way only Paxton McLemore could overtake her body and her mind so completely.

His increasingly hard thrusts sent her into a tailspin and she screamed her release as he surged against her. In this moment, need, relief and love rolled into one, leaving no more room for the fear.

Twelve

It took a moment for Paxton to realize that Ivy was quiet, not moving as he parked in front of Auntie's house. Despite the physical connection forged in his office last week, they'd tiptoed around each other and the heavy subjects neither of them seemed to want to tackle.

Paxton knew Ivy was afraid for the future, but he had no answers for her, despite their incredible attraction. So he left the emotions locked away, where they were safe. Where he was safe. She seemed content to do the same.

Still, every time they touched, those emotions made an appearance.

"Are you okay, Ivy?" he asked, a little worried by the way she stared out the window, toward her family home without making a move to get out of the car.

Then there was the way she worried her lower lip with her teeth. That little move told him something weighed on her mind. He wanted to ignore it, to avoid any deep subject that would upset their current intimate equilibrium. But he wasn't a coward, especially not with the women he cared about.

Ignoring the jolt of that thought, Paxton pressed harder. "What is it, sweetheart?" he asked.

She glanced his way with the weak smile. "Just hormonal, I guess."

"That doesn't make it any less valid," he reassured her, only to be reminded of his words to his sister last week. He'd forgotten in the upset at the office and its aftermath to check on Sierra. He needed to do that.

"I love my sisters," Ivy finally said. "I'm so excited that I'm finally feeling well enough to help Jasmine with this charity auction." She worried her lips with her teeth some more. As sexy as he found that...

"But..." he prompted.

"Sometimes it's hard to be with them." He caught a brief glimpse of a sad smile. "They're so happy. They have strong relationships. They're building families. And I have..." She frowned. "What? A business relationship? With an extra helping of sex?"

Her pain and uncertainty hit him hard. Hard enough to overcome his reluctance to go deeper. "No, Ivy." He cupped her worried face between his palms and struggled for honesty. "I'm not sure exactly what this is between us—yet—but the last thing I want is a business arrangement. Hell, especially not in the office."

The smile they shared was more intimate than Paxton could ever remember having with any other woman.

But the feeling faded as she asked, "So why are you holding back?"

He was. He knew that, knew it came not just from the obstacles with his family, but his own memories of being used by a woman in the past, something he wasn't ready to talk about. So he deflected. "Why are you?"

The knowledge was there in her eyes, even though he knew she didn't want to admit it. "We both have reasons for holding back, Ivy."

Leaving it at that, he got out of the car and went around to open her door.

He genuinely enjoyed dinner with her family, appreciating how open and welcoming they were to him and to each other. There was no strategy in the way they interacted, no subtle attempt to one-up each other. Paxton could relax and be himself.

After the meal, Royce left to attend a meeting, and the women got down to the business of planning the upcoming auction that Jasmine was coordinating through her event-planner business.

Paxton spent some time reading about the history of Savannah's shipping industry in the books on the overcrowded bookshelves in the front parlor. It was fascinating to learn more about the industry his family had been involved in since they'd settled in Savannah so long ago. Then he chatted with Auntie until she fell asleep in front of the television.

He was certainly living the high life tonight.

Finally he decided it was time to at least check in and see how much longer the women would be working. He headed back down the hall from the front parlor to the kitchen, Auntie's snores fading into the background. The women's conversation was muffled until he reached the doorway to the dining room.

Only then did some of Willow's muffled words take shape. "Oh, they were more than happy to talk... just not about that night."

Paxton paused, confusion running through him.

Willow went on, "He never said...never out right admitted his involvement. So while it's likely he was involved...ship, there's no proof..."

Icy shock jolted through Paxton's body. His brain struggled to catch up. He strained to hear more.

"But don't give up, Ivy. Tate will find something."

"What should I do in the meantime? After the... office, I'm afraid...if they find out before we have proof."

Willow sniffed. "I'd watch that grandmother of his... She hears the name Kane, and it's all over."

Kane. It sounded so familiar, but Paxton probably wouldn't have realized why if Willow hadn't paired it with his grandmother. *The ship.*

Kane was the name of the man who had sunk his family's ship.

Cold rational logic was the only thing to get him through this. He stepped into the kitchen to a chorus of gasps all around.

"Ivy, what exactly is it that you know about the Kane family?"

She swallowed hard, but then lifted her chin and replied, "That was my mother's maiden name."

Fury bubbled up from his core before Paxton shut it down through sheer will. "So, you deliberately kept this from me?"

She didn't answer, but her wide eyes remained trained on him as he stepped closer.

"Is this one of those 'things I'm going to hide from you because I don't have a direction yet' scenarios? The kind that keep me protected until you can decide exactly what *you* want to do?"

Ivy cast a quick, guilty glance toward her sisters before she slowly nodded. "Maybe. But, Paxton—"

He cut her off with a sharp, dismissive wave of his hand. "You were talking about the sinking of a ship. The one that took the McLemores' heir and beloved son from them?" Paxton's angry words rang through the kitchen. He thought back over what little he'd heard. "That night is a scar on my family's heritage. My grandmother has never been the same since that night."

The rest of the earlier conversation slowly registered.

"What makes you think this man you were talking about was responsible?" he asked as he put two and two together. He ignored their shocked faces as he stepped farther into the room. "Even more, why would you care?"

"Paxton—" Ivy swallowed.

Ivy was part of the Kane family. The implications hit hard and fast. He stomped closer. "I want to know what's going on, Ivy," he said, pinning her with his hard stare. "Right now."

Her mouth worked, but it took a minute for words to come out. "Paxton, I didn't want you to find out—"

"Obviously. I realize you're not that familiar with my family, but the story of that ship is notorious. My grandmother tells it often. It was devastating to our family."

He circled around to get a better look at her face. "But to my knowledge, the family that was responsible left Savannah. The Kanes. Isn't that right, Ivy?"

She slowly shook her head. "It's not what you think, Paxton."

"Are you sure? Because it sounds to me like you are part of a family that attacked our company *and* our family."

Paxton knew he sounded overly emotional about something that happened generations ago. But that was just how sensitive his grandmother was over the same subject. It had shaped the McLemores' entire history.

Jasmine stepped in. "Yes, Paxton. We are descendants of the Kane family that was accused of sinking that ship. But that's not—"

"No, I want to hear it from her." He leaned against the table, so heavily that the pattern of the wood grain registered against his palms. "Have you known this all along and hidden it from me, Ivy?"

"Yes," she said, finally meeting his gaze. "I have known all along, Paxton."

"And once again, you chose not to tell me?"

Willow answered. "You'd never have given her a job in the first place."

Another cold shock wave washed over him. "So, you knew *before* you came to work for me?"

"I did know, but it wasn't important because my family didn't do it."

"Like hell they didn't."

Both women took to their feet at that point, speaking over each other. Paxton waved it all away and focused solely on Ivy.

"You could have told me at any time, but you didn't because…why would you even come to work for me when you knew…"

He wasn't buying her broken expression or her silence.

"Did you think if I knew that I would have come within ten feet of you?"

Confirmation of what he'd said came in the expression on her face, in the crocodile tears that trickled down her creamy cheeks. "I needed a job…well, wanted a good job. Yours was a great opportunity. I didn't think you would ever know."

"Now I do," Paxton said, letting his anger free as he leaned in close to her face. "You're right… I wouldn't touch a Kane if you paid me."

He turned on his heel and made a beeline for the door, his hard steps accompanied by furious whispers and quiet sobs. But he ignored it all as he shot back over his shoulder.

"There's something you might want to remember, dear Ivy—my family would be more than happy to run yours out of town for a second time."

"I don't know, Tate," Ivy said as she stared at the modern-fairy-tale facade of Paxton's house. "I don't want it to look like I'm throwing around my family's new connections."

She'd never seen Paxton so angry before, even when he'd learned about the baby. The very intensity of his emotions had frozen her in place.

He'd stormed out last night, leaving Ivy stranded at Auntie's house. Her sisters had consoled her with chocolate and ginger ale, since she shouldn't have wine, but she was determined to talk to him today, especially before he contacted the family lawyer about custody. It was a weekend, but she doubted the lawyer would refuse calls from him at any time. With as many connections as the McLemores had, they probably had their attorney's home number on speed dial.

But as she sat in the driveway, she second-guessed her decision to come here with Tate. Even after such a short time, the house looked like it was waiting for her. So perfect. And now everything had fallen apart. What good would convincing Paxton of her family's innocence do?

All she knew was that she couldn't leave things the way they'd ended last night.

Paxton didn't look any happier when he opened the

door for them. "Have you come to get your stuff? Or just to spread more lies?"

Tate stepped into view. He didn't have to say anything, just stand firm.

Paxton glanced between them. "Back-up?"

Tate shrugged. "Call it whatever you want. But let's have a civil discussion before any decisions are made."

For a moment Ivy thought Paxton would refuse. But he finally stepped back and let them inside.

She followed him into one of the front rooms, staring at his stiff back. Then he turned to brace himself. Arms crossed over his chest. Legs locked. Anger closing off his expression.

Ivy struggled to clear her throat. "Paxton, this is Tate Kingston. Willow's fiancé."

Paxton arched a brow in recognition at Tate's name before closing his expression down tight. "Start talking," he said.

Tate grunted a protest, but Ivy held up her hand.

"I'm not going to apologize for not telling you about this up-front," she said, using all of her control to keep her voice steady. "It wasn't important when I first came to work for you. It was more important that I was good at my job and you needed help in the office. Besides, I didn't plan to get close…" She took a deep breath. They both knew how those first intentions had been derailed. "Then you left. There just wasn't time to address it."

"What about since I came home? There's no excuse for not telling me, Ivy."

"Really?" She took a few steps closer, her heart pounding hard enough to bring on a wave of nausea. "Knowing how your family feels about mine, would you honestly place a child in the middle of that?"

She could tell her question hit home, but he quickly shrugged it off. "That doesn't change the fact that your family is guilty."

"Maybe they aren't," Tate said as he stepped forward. "I want you to look at this."

Paxton threw her a quick glance she couldn't read, then focused on Tate and the worn ledger in his hands.

"Your family and the Kanes weren't the only successful shipping families in the area at the time. Mine was also around. The Kingston family was ruthlessly undercutting the competition in an attempt to take over the majority of the business in and out of Savannah's ports," Tate said. "Now, I don't know what evidence caused your family to focus on the Kanes, especially after the police cleared them, but I think mine is a little more compelling."

Tate laid the book on the coffee table and opened it to a page not quite halfway through. "Do you recognize this date?"

Paxton gave the page a quick glance, then paused for a longer look. "Yes." He drew the word out.

"This ledger is the place my great-great-grandfather kept record of all of his business transactions that were…let's just say, illegal. To put it mildly."

Paxton raised a brow, giving him a look as princely as his surroundings. "I'm surprised you keep this."

"Why wouldn't I?" Tate shrugged. "The Kingstons

have always thought they were invincible. Every generation of them. All of the family records are stored on the third floor of Sabatini House, much to Willow's delight."

Paxton tilted his head in question.

"She's quite the history buff."

Tate's casual manner seemed to calm Paxton a little. Much to Ivy's relief.

His stance relaxed somewhat as he listened intently to the rest of Tate's story. "It did not surprise me to know that my ancestors were not very nice people. I knew from personal experience. I'm not exaggerating when I say they were ruthless in their business dealings. I can assure you, it was not much different in their personal endeavors."

"Are you actually proud of these criminals?" Paxton asked with an incredulous shake of his head.

"Absolutely not. They were bastards, by my standards. But it does make for interesting book fodder."

Ivy might have smiled if the situation hadn't been so tense. Only Tate, a famous horror author, would look at it that way.

Paxton looked a little dazed himself.

"Anyway, Willow found this in the attic and the date does correlate with the sinking of the McLemore ship."

Paxton crossed his arms over his chest again, closing himself off. "Well, this is quite convenient for her."

Fear pierced Ivy's chest. What if Tate's plan didn't work? She hadn't realized just how much hope had risen in her heart since Tate had started talking. Could she handle it if everything stayed sour between her and Paxton?

Tate didn't seem at all phased by the remark. "The investigation was purely an academic exercise until Ivy's, well, predicament came along."

Great, now Paxton was back to shooting daggers in her direction. Metaphorically, of course.

Tate just kept talking. "We knew it would be important to find out what really happened, if we could. For the baby's sake, if nothing else."

"That doesn't explain why I wasn't told."

Ivy stepped up, though her tight throat made speaking hard. "And I may never be able to explain it. I'm sorry, Paxton. I had to make a lot of tough decisions on my own. You might have made a different choice. But remember, it's easier from the outside, looking in."

He stiffened.

"Besides," Tate said, "we thought we'd have more proof of her family's innocence by now. I contacted the family of the man who signed the contract with my relatives, but they weren't able to offer more than confirmation of his shady character."

"But no specifics about the ship?"

"No. Not only would he never mention it, he left the room if it came up in any conversation."

That tidbit seemed suspicious in and of itself. "How would they know that?"

"Family legend," Tate supplied. "They passed down the story that on his deathbed, he tried to tell them something. The only word he could utter was

McLemore. His surviving family members suspected he'd been involved somehow and remembered his odd behavior. But they were never able to get a confirmation from him."

Paxton turned away, but not before Ivy noticed a slight shake in his hands. Hope surged as she held her breath.

After several long, silent moments, he turned back to face them. "You have the most to lose, Tate. Do you believe this?" He waved a hand toward the ledger.

"Wholeheartedly. But there's nothing to lose for me. I don't care what people think of me or my family. My future wife and sisters-in-law are another matter."

Ivy wanted to hug her future brother-in-law, but she was too busy wondering if the actual evidence was enough to give her a fighting chance.

Thirteen

Paxton could understand Tate's sentiment—all too well.

It would be easy to quit caring about his family and be led by his fascination with Ivy. He should have spent the night figuring out how to sue for custody of his child. Instead he'd spent the hours obsessing over losing the woman who had come to mean so much to him.

So much about Ivy had haunted his dreams. Her sexy lips and enthusiasm in bed. Her hard work and ability to handle all manner of issues in the office. Her love for her family, which rivalled his own. Then there was the incredible fact that his child grew inside of her, spawned by a night of passion he'd never forget. Not a single moment.

But he'd been lied to by pretty faces before. He wasn't sure he could get over that.

"So," Tate said as he gathered up the ledger. "This portion of the investigation is at a dead end. But we're still looking for clues."

"Have you thought about a private detective?"

Tate shook his head. "I don't know where they'd look except where we are already looking. And I don't want a stranger poking around my house."

The thought still niggled at Paxton. Maybe...

"So...can I leave you two alone, or do I need to go get some packing boxes?"

Paxton couldn't bring himself to look at Ivy just yet, but he noticed her body shift in his peripheral vision.

Did he want to do this? Was what they had together worth working this out for? Or should he walk away while he still could? Before he revealed more about himself than he felt comfortable with.

His body shouted *yes, keep her.* But his mind knew exactly where this conversation with Ivy would lead. She would be just as demanding for answers as he had been. He wasn't sure he was ready to reveal so much about himself or if he could handle how close it might bring them.

Again he noticed that slight movement out of the corner of his eyes as the minutes ticked by. What did he want? Then a soft feeling of contentment invaded his chest and he knew what he needed to do.

"Give us some time, Tate," Paxton said. "We can call if Ivy needs you."

Tate stared him down for a long moment. Clearly taking his measure. Paxton let him. He had to take into account that two pretty high-powered men had become involved with Ivy's family. Tate wanted to know if he could trust Paxton. He would want to know the same if they were talking about one of Paxton's sisters.

"Okay," Tate conceded. "Ivy?"

As Paxton turned his gaze in her direction, she nodded.

"You have my cell phone number." The front door closed after Tate, leaving behind the most awkward silence Paxton had ever experienced.

Ivy didn't hesitate to break it. "I'm sorry, Paxton."

"I know." And somehow he did. How he'd become this attuned to her, he wasn't sure. The connection wasn't always clear when his emotions got in the way. Still the certainty remained.

"I needed to protect myself. My family. But I realize now how selfish it was of me to hide this from you after we became...involved. I just thought I could fix it first."

The strained tone in her voice pulled his reluctant glance her way—just in time to see her tilt slightly off-balance.

"Ivy, sit down."

He ushered her into a nearby armchair. As soon as she was seated firmly in place, he forced himself to step away. He could see the hurt on her face, but couldn't admit he had to pull back before he pulled her close.

Instead he channeled all of his chaotic thoughts and resulting pent-up energy into a steady bout of pacing. "I don't know, Ivy. I don't know if I can get past this."

"The family thing—"

"The hiding. The secrets."

It was a long moment of silence. Paxton couldn't speak. His hypocrisy suddenly hit him hard, and his stomach dipped as though in anticipation of riding a roller coaster. How could he talk about her secrets when he insisted on keeping his own? Could he really do this? Expose his humiliating history to her?

"I'm only going to say this one more time. I'm sorry, Paxton." Ivy's voice was harder than he'd ever heard it. Justifiably so. "I should have told you what I knew."

"That seems like a running theme with you." Maybe he still had some anger lurking beneath the surface. Then again, emotions were rarely cut-and-dried.

"Look, I get that you're angry, but you also don't have stories handed down from your parents of your great-grandfather being so terrified after someone runs his wife's car off the road with his baby daughter inside that he packs up their bags and flees during the middle of the night to protect his family."

That stopped his pacing in an instant. "What?"

"Guess your grandmother left that part out, huh?" Ivy's eyes were glistening. Her face scrunched up with emotion. Paxton couldn't look away. "That was just the last in a long line of terror that was dished out to him before they ran for their lives. I know exactly what your family is capable of."

He should, too. He'd suspected they had resorted to physical violence, but the details were never shared. To hurt an innocent woman and her child was unthinkable.

"If there was an option for proving our innocence, I wanted to take it, Paxton."

And his family, the one he'd been trying so hard to serve, were the ones who had pushed her to keep the truth from him. Paxton felt all of his preconceived notions start to crack.

"I really do understand, Paxton," she said, pushing up from her chair and crossing the room to him. Each step had a hesitancy to it, as if she weren't quite sure she should approach. "And I wanted to trust you. But I wasn't ready. At first it honestly didn't matter. But later, with the baby, there was too much at stake."

She laid a hand on his arm. "I know you were caught off guard. But I thought we were getting to know each other. Why wouldn't you even listen to me? Give me a chance to explain?"

In that moment his gaze lifted and he caught sight of those gorgeous blue eyes and the stunning amount of hurt they held.

"I will not live through that again," she insisted. "Paxton, I know I didn't tell you right away, but that's not lying. About this or the baby. I can't always tell you every single thing according to your timetable. I just can't."

He was already shaking his head, knowing his own

secrets would have to be revealed. It was the only way to fix this problem.

"It's not about you. It comes from someone before you." His throat closed, as if urging him to keep his secrets to himself. To spare himself from reliving the humiliation. But she deserved something, even if it was only the bare facts. He had to look away from her fixed gaze.

"I was involved with someone, a long time ago." He couldn't tell her how infatuated he'd been, how naive. He'd grown up fast in the end. "I was young and stupid. I overlooked a lot of clues that I was being used before I overheard her telling her friends that she was with me for my money."

He expected a sympathetic look or maybe even a few tears, but instead anger transformed Ivy's face.

"Seriously? How could someone, anyone, get to know you and still only want you for your money? How pathetically shallow could she be?"

Her surprising outrage dissolved his embarrassment in seconds. That wasn't at all what he'd expected...though he might have if he'd been thinking with any kind of clarity. He was still uncomfortable with what he'd shared, but she deserved the truth after he'd been so judgmental.

"At least you're good for my ego," he said with a slight laugh.

She studied him as if she knew he wasn't telling her everything, knew there was something deeper behind his quip, but she didn't press for more.

Instead she shook her head. "Paxton, I'm so sorry.

I just didn't know when the right time was to tell you everything."

"Do I know it all now?"

To his surprise, she met his gaze head-on. "You know everything I know." Her sigh echoed his own exhaustion. "I just don't want to put my family in any jeopardy. They don't deserve that."

Immediate protests rose to his lips, but he held them back. As much as he didn't want to admit it to himself, she had a right to be afraid.

He wasn't sure what his family would do when they found out the truth. He still wasn't sure what he felt about it himself. He only knew that he couldn't turn his back on this woman for something that happened to his family several generations ago. Or for something that happened to him when he was just a kid.

Right then and there, he determined to get himself out of the past long enough to appreciate what might just be his future. But he had a feeling his family wouldn't follow suit.

Paxton listened intently to the shower running in the master suite, wishing he could join Ivy under the warm rush of water. Technically things between them had returned to normal on the surface, but the underlying strain of uncertainty kept them from truly coming together.

The ease Paxton had started to feel with Ivy had disappeared. He found he missed it, even though he'd told himself they shouldn't get close. There wasn't a clear way forward on their relationship after the revelations about her family. He should keep his distance.

But the deep, aching need for her didn't follow any logic. Listening to the shower running, thinking of joining her in it, was torture.

His moment of indecision was solved when the doorbell rang. Paxton felt a brief panic. The house was in a gated community, so his visitor wasn't going to be a random salesman. His neighbors rarely came over. Those interactions usually came at unexpected moments, when they were out in their yards. It could very well be one of his relatives, though they'd rarely been here since he'd moved in. Then what would he do?

As the bell rang again, Paxton knew he couldn't ignore it. All the lights were on. No one would buy that he wasn't home. So he opened the door and found Sierra on his doorstep.

He hurried to relieve her of the heavy toddler draped over her growing belly. "Sierra, what are you doing here?" he asked, panic truly taking hold. What should he do about Ivy? He had no way to warn her.

His niece wrapped her arms around his neck and snuggled close. The drive must've made her sleepy. Then Sierra stepped inside and the light glittered over the tears on her cheeks.

"What's wrong?" Everything left his mind in that moment except helping his sister.

"I just don't know what to do anymore, Paxton."

A vision of Alicia in his office flashed through his mind. *I just wondered if you had noticed anything off with Sierra?*

"Tell me what happened," he urged her.

"It's like he's decided I'm invisible or something." She waved her arms around to emphasize her point. "I wake up and he's gone. He doesn't come home until after I'm in bed. Honestly, if it wasn't for the dirty dishes, I wouldn't even know he'd been there."

More tears spilled over.

"You haven't spoken to him about this at all?" He led her through the front hallway to the breakfast nook.

"I haven't seen the man in a week."

That wasn't good. What husband went a whole week without seeing his pregnant wife and daughter? This had to be something serious, or she was right: he'd completely lost interest.

He got Sierra settled into a chair, then eased into another one himself and leaned back so that his niece could lie more comfortably. It was well past the toddler's bedtime. What would Sierra's husband think when he came home to an empty house?

Paxton gave a heavy sigh, then jumped in with the most obvious question. "Do you think he's cheating?"

Sierra slowly shook her head. "I don't think so. Otherwise why bother to come home at all? I mean, yes, his clothes are there, but he could take them with him at any time. It's not like I do the laundry."

"Do you think maybe he's worried about something? About a project at work? His move on the board? What about his family?"

Sierra frowned for a moment, then shrugged. "Well, I don't know."

Though the McLemores made marital decisions based on logic, and what was best for the family and the company, that didn't mean that the relationships were cold or heartless. Sierra and her husband had formed a merger, but they got along well enough to produce two children.

"We never really talked about that," Sierra continued. "You know, problems or what's going on at work."

Hmm… "What do you talk about?"

"Her," she said, nodding toward her daughter.

"What about before she came along?"

"Well, we were building the house, and I guess mutual acquaintances. We went out to a lot of parties."

Paxton was beginning to see part of the problem. It might not be the complete issue, but it was definitely a start.

"Maybe you should talk to him," he suggested, thinking back over his and Ivy's own issues. "If you haven't let him know that he can come to you if there's a problem, then why would he?"

His own words hit him with a jolt. Was that how Ivy had felt? Like she couldn't come to him because he wouldn't care enough? Because he would always side with his family over her? Especially after he'd left. He felt like such a dolt.

With a little frown, Sierra said, "I guess that's true."

Paxton leaned forward, but was careful not to jostle his precious bundle too much. "Do you want to stay? Or is this marriage not what you want anymore?"

Sierra glanced away, the frown becoming more pronounced. She absently rubbed her distended belly. "I guess I wouldn't be upset if I didn't really want this. Right?"

"So, this isn't just hormones? Or some kind of possessiveness thing rearing its head?"

"No." She looked up and held his gaze. "No, it's not."

As soon as the words were out, she raised her brows at him as if asking for his approval. But she didn't need it. He reached across to squeeze her hand, which had finally come to rest on the table. "If it's what you want, then maybe you should start fighting for it instead of just wondering and worrying."

She opened her mouth to respond, but suddenly her gaze snapped to the doorway behind him. "Who is that?"

It took Paxton a minute to realize what was happening. He glanced over his shoulder to see Ivy in the kitchen. She had a pretty cotton nightgown on and a towel wrapped around her damp hair as she looked into the refrigerator.

How on earth could he have forgotten about her?

"Is that a woman?" Sierra headed to the kitchen with a grin. Paxton was slow to follow, hampered as he was by the toddler hanging on him.

"Hey, there." But Sierra's voice trailed off as Ivy turned around, her eyes bright blue and wide.

"Paxton!" his sister said, her gaze darting between the two of them. "Are you sleeping with your secretary?"

Fourteen

Over the next week, Ivy waited anxiously for the other shoe to drop. Though Paxton assured her he'd sworn his sister to secrecy, she knew it was only a matter of time before word got back to his family that a woman was living in his house.

That would probably be worse for them than just knowing that he'd slept with her. Living here implied some kind of permanency. How humiliating would it be to listen to Paxton explain the uncertainty of their current arrangement?

She was just thankful it had been Sierra who had walked in that night, rather than Alicia. The latter was a mini-replica of Paxton's mother, Elizabeth, neither of whom were the nicest women to deal with. Sierra, on the other hand, tended to be more personable. It helped that she usually had her little girl when she came into the office, which lightened things up quite a bit.

But Sierra's surprise, and referring to Ivy as Paxton's assistant, had left Ivy in no mood to talk that night. Not to mention being caught in her pj's. Startled, Ivy had rushed out of the kitchen and into the downstairs bedroom, staying inside until Paxton joined her almost an hour later.

Listening to him talk about Sierra's visit had made the lack of a heads-up much more understandable. Yes, Paxton could have excused himself for a quick trip to the bathroom and warned Ivy to stay upstairs. But her tears had tripped Paxton into big-brother mode, ready to help Sierra slay any dragons that she needed help with.

While Ivy hated that Sierra was having trouble with her relationship, she was more worried about what her little visit to Paxton's house would mean for Ivy. And eventually Ivy's baby.

It only took a week to find out.

The morning had been slow and smooth in the office. Paxton had no meetings he had to attend. They were making steady progress until Paxton had a conference call, so Ivy settled in to work up some notes he'd asked her for. The part-time assistant would come in that afternoon so Ivy could go home to rest. Paxton had insisted, because she hadn't been sleeping well.

She hadn't had the heart to tell him it was worry keeping her awake, not her pregnancy.

The quiet morning made Elizabeth McLemore's arrival all the more jarring. Her appearance was usually a no-brainer. Though she was a forceful woman, she understood having to wait while Paxton was in a meeting or on the phone. Her words to Ivy were always short and to the point, making their interactions easy, even if they were uncomfortable on Ivy's part.

Today was a whole other matter. Her march through the door and trained gaze set off a wave of nausea for Ivy. Still she pasted on a smile and said, "He's on a phone call, Mrs. McLemore, but I'll message that you're here."

"No need. I'm not here to see him."

"Excuse me?" Ivy was horrified to hear her voice come out as a squeak.

Paxton's mother raised a haughty brow as if that little noise just confirmed her superiority. "I just want to know if there is something you hope to gain by sleeping with my son?"

Keep it a secret, my foot. So much for Sierra keeping her mouth shut. Ivy raised herself slowly to her feet, even though her body suddenly felt like lead, in hopes it would help her project confidence. "Mrs. McLemore, what happens between Paxton and I—"

"Is of complete interest to me, since I serve on this company's board."

"Why?" For a moment Ivy didn't quite understand the correlation. "You're going to reprimand your son for being involved with his assistant?"

"No. Not my son."

Ivy had only a moment to absorb the panic that

streaked through her. Thankfully Paxton opened his door. Taking a page from Alicia's book, Ivy asked, "Are you threatening me?" Petty, but she wanted Paxton to hear exactly what was happening. For himself.

"Ivy—Mother. What's going on here?"

Suddenly his mother was all smiles. "Darling, your sister was telling me about your new—well, I came down to meet her."

Ivy cocked her head to the side. "I've worked here for a year and a half. You've met me before," she insisted.

His mother ignored her, as usual. "Sierra tried to tell me, but I knew you would have told me first."

Paxton didn't seem as concerned as Ivy would like. Deep inside, panic tightened her every muscle.

"You wouldn't have listened," he said simply.

"I always have time for—"

"You wouldn't have listened, because you wouldn't like what you heard."

Startled, Ivy noticed a deepening of his tone, as if something hidden was slowly coming to the surface.

"Ivy was at my house by my choice. Our choice. And it's nobody's business but ours until we are ready to share it. I simply wanted to wait until I knew there was something to tell."

"Is there? Because Sierra seemed to think this person, your assistant, was living with you." Her gaze shot straight over to Ivy as if she could not believe that would be true.

"I believe so," Paxton said quietly.

The odd note in his voice had Ivy looking his way.

He looked back, his expression oddly hopeful. Hesitant. In that moment it was as if all the recent distance between them had dissolved. The connection of their gazes suddenly had a sizzle, as if her psyche had just been waiting for his to accept what they both knew was happening between them.

"I'm sure Miss Baxter will be very disappointed," Elizabeth said sotto voce.

"Through no fault of mine."

"Yes, well…" Obviously she didn't agree. Her expression tightened, with tiny frown lines appearing, along with a slight curl to her lip. "We shall see."

She turned to the door, but Paxton stopped her. "Did you need to see me, Mother?"

Her gaze flicked to Ivy. "No. I got what I came for."

She was almost out the door when she turned back again, causing Ivy's stomach to lurch. She was definitely gonna need the afternoon off.

"I almost forgot, your grandmother expects to see you at the luncheon on Sunday. Both of you." Her eyes widened in an innocent expression that Ivy wasn't buying. "See you then."

"Welcome."

Alicia spoke with the appropriate formality, but the Cheshire grin was what had him worried. For the first time, he found himself on guard against his own family.

Protective instincts swelled inside him. Not for his child, as he would have expected, but for Ivy.

The unfamiliarity of it itched just beneath his Sunday suit. Still he couldn't deny what it was. Without hesitation he laid his hand at the small of her back—a move of both possession and solidarity. Beneath his palm, her muscles relaxed just a touch.

An echo of the heat he felt whenever he was alone with her flashed through him, pulling him even closer to her.

They moved through the grand foyer, with its strategically hung chandelier, skylights and oversize palm plants placed for dramatic affect. Paxton turned left into the library where he knew the rest of the family would be having drinks.

Sierra was the first to meet him. "I'm sorry, Paxton," she whispered as she slipped into his arms for a solid hug.

Leave it to Sierra to head a scolding off at the pass. She even turned to the woman at his side and said, "Welcome, Ivy," her voice much warmer than Alicia's had been.

Paxton shook hands with Sierra's husband, who offered a somewhat strained smile before slipping an arm around her. Paxton noted the move with surprise. One thing Sierra and Jason had never exhibited was any kind of affection in public. None whatsoever. But as he watched his sister slowly relax into the touch, he hoped this was a result of a much-needed come-to-Jesus meeting. Whatever brought happiness to his sister was worth it.

Determined to give the right impression immediately, he cupped Ivy's arm possessively and led her to where the elder McLemores congregated. They didn't bother to stand, which made him frown.

"Mother, you know Ivy. Father, this is Ivy Harden, whom I don't believe you've had the pleasure of meeting."

His father had the class to get up and bow over Ivy's hand. Father's manners had always been impeccable.

"Grandmother, this is Ivy Harden. Ivy, Karen McLemore."

Beneath his touch, Ivy stiffened as his grandmother nodded her head in a regal gesture, then returned to the conversation without any other acknowledgment. Paxton used his hold to pull Ivy closer into his heat, seeking to comfort her.

His grandmother knew exactly what she was doing. Her social persona was second nature; he'd seen it in action his whole life. Snubbing Ivy was her way of getting her point across—this person wasn't welcome, even though she'd been commanded to be here.

Paxton suddenly wished he'd followed his instincts and left Ivy at home, confronting his family on his own. Less collateral damage.

Because Grandmother had just made it clear she was up to something. But what approach would she take? Mulling it over, he guided Ivy over to the younger set and joined their conversation.

When dinner was served, Ivy barely ate under his grandmother's stare in the formal dining room. Paxton started to worry the nausea, which hadn't made an appearance in days, had returned.

Conversation was smooth for the first half of the meal, but his grandmother remained silent, upping the tension.

"So, Paxton—" Grandmother's voice echoed around the walls when she finally spoke "—what can you tell me about this young lady?"

Paxton was startled by the question, but decided it was in their best interest to simply answer. "Well, Ivy has been my assistant for almost two years, and keeps the office running better than anyone before her."

Paxton noticed that Ivy simply gave up eating, and dropped her hands to her lap. But she refused to be cowed. Instead she kept her head high with a polite smile on her face.

"And your family, dear? I don't believe I've heard of them."

Paxton stiffened. There was no way his sister could've known who Ivy's family really was. And Paxton was not ready to start World War Three over it until he had more information.

Ivy answered the question with a simple, "I'm orphaned, actually."

"A secretary and an orphan. Well, isn't that just pitiful."

It should have sounded sympathetic, but it didn't. Paxton narrowed his eyes toward his grandmother.

"From what I understand of your family, you're solidly middle class."

Ivy turned her head slowly to meet Paxton's gaze,

giving him a clear view of her resignation before she once again faced the head of the table.

"We make do… But if you knew that about my family, *Karen*, then why did you ask me about them?"

"A simple fishing expedition, my dear. A family like ours must keep protections in place."

"Protections?" Ivy shook her head. "Isn't that a bit melodramatic? You seem pretty well protected to me."

"Oh, one can never be too protected from people like you."

A sudden stillness invaded the room, causing Paxton's voice to echo off the walls. "Grandmother, that's enough."

"I'm sorry, Paxton. You brought this on yourself."

"What?"

"I never took you for being so gullible. Then again, pretty faces are your weakness. They always have been."

Anger shot straight through Paxton at the reference, pushing him to his feet. "I said, that's enough." The burn of regret flooded his chest. "Let's go, Ivy."

As he helped Ivy up from her chair, Karen said, "So, you would disregard your family's prudent warning in favor of a woman who will trick you into marrying her?"

This time the gasp was more collective. Paxton was glad to see some of his family had sensibilities.

"I have never demanded that Paxton marry me," Ivy insisted.

"But that baby gives you a pretty good meal ticket,

at least for the next eighteen to twenty-two years, in my opinion."

Paxton froze for a moment. Ivy's soft whimper seemed loud in the room. How his grandmother had found out about the baby, he wasn't sure.

"She's pregnant?" his mother moaned.

A quick glance showed each of his sisters eyeing each other with raised brows. The rest of the audience was frozen in place, not daring to interfere, though his father did shoot him a look of sympathy.

He wanted to get Ivy out of there fast, but knew retreat would be seen as weakness by his family. He'd have to stick it out a little longer.

"Though I don't know how you know that, Ivy did not trick me into getting pregnant. I'm the one who provided the protection." If the situation hadn't been so tense, Paxton would have smiled as he remembered the illuminating conversation with Auntie.

His mother's face scrunched up. "Paxton!"

"Grandmother brought it up. I'm simply stating the truth."

But the elder Mrs. McLemore wasn't buying it. "I'm sure that's what she let you think. Regardless the result is the same." Karen folded her hands before her as if reinforcing her matriarch status. Her words were clear and even. "Despite how it came about, the first male grandchild will be a wonderful addition to our family."

"What?" Ivy said, confusion clouding her face. "I thought you didn't want anything to do with me?"

Paxton reached out for her arm. He had a feeling it wasn't going to be that easy.

"Regardless of whether we marry or not, Ivy and her baby will be a wonderful addition to the McLemore family," he said.

"Hardly, Paxton. I'm afraid we must maintain standards." She eyed Ivy. "But that's all right—everyone has a price."

Ivy's entire body snapped to attention. Paxton could tell by the hard look on her face that she'd had enough. He had, too. Unfortunately his grandmother spoke before he could get them moving toward the door.

"So, how much is it, my dear? I'm sure a lawyer will happily draw up an agreement for us to purchase your parental rights."

Ivy scoffed, even as her face went sheet white. "There isn't enough money in the world to separate me from my child, lady. Especially not after all I've been through."

The pain on her face shook Paxton to his core. Time to end this.

He stepped in close and secured her to his side with her arm through his; a look was all he could give her right now to assure her he understood. Then he escorted her to the head of the table, where he paused to look down at his grandmother, his body a barrier meant to protect Ivy.

"All I asked for was a number, Paxton," Karen said, an odd look of surprise in her amber eyes, so much like his own. How could she not know what she was doing was wrong?

He'd happily set her straight. "Since you obviously haven't realized this yet, let me make a few things clear. One. Ivy and I will make our own decisions in this situation. Not you. Not Mother or Father."

Then he leaned closer, dominating his grandmother's space in a way he never had before. "And two, if you think I'm the type of man to separate any woman from her child, you never knew me at all."

Fifteen

Concern for Ivy exploded in Paxton's chest on the drive back to his house. When they got inside, defeat weighed her down, causing her to sag against the side table in the foyer, her head hanging forward. Paxton sympathized. She'd been through so much. His family's behavior had to be a body blow.

One he didn't know how to soften...even for himself.

Without hesitation he put his arms around her, pressing himself firmly against her back as if to protect her from another hit. "It will be okay, Ivy," he whispered against her temple.

Though he didn't know how. He knew his grandmother well. If her decision about Ivy was this firm, she'd just keep coming. She didn't back down. Weakness was a trait she'd never allowed to fester, not even at her advanced age.

Could he possibly find a way to change her mind?

Unbidden, he found himself swaying back and forth as if to music only he could hear. Slowly Ivy's body softened, the tension leaching away. He drew her even closer against him, wishing they were skin to skin. But the lack of space in the foyer was almost symbolic to him—the two of them, together as one against the world. Most power struggles were simply a business game to him—a cat-and-mouse race to see who reached the prize first. Winning was a pleasure.

Now it was a necessity. For him. For Ivy. For their child.

"We'll get through this together."

Together. They would, but right now there would be no fighting. Only love.

Yes. That was what they needed.

He lifted her into his arms, savoring her gasp of surprise. Then he carried her up the stairs to the master suite. His room. Their room.

And he wanted nothing more than to have this princess in his bed.

It was a little reminiscent of a fairy tale, he had to admit. The thought made him grin, a return of lightness. Though she didn't come from an upper-class background, Ivy had always reminded him of a princess. It was just in the air about her and the way she held herself. As he laid her in the king-size bed, her golden hair spread across the burgundy-colored pillows, giving her a rich, royal air.

The impression didn't diminish as he removed her clothing, piece by piece. If anything, the white lace bra and panties gave her an even more noble air. How anyone could look at Ivy, with her classic bone structure and regal demeanor, and define her as something common was beyond him.

He wanted to tell her how gorgeous, how perfect she was. Instead he determined to show her.

Quickly Paxton stripped his tie and jacket, toeing off his shoes while he opened his shirt one button at a time. He held her gaze, letting the anticipation build.

Ivy had been the adventure of a lifetime.

Needing to be closer, he crawled up, letting the open sides of his shirt fall on either side of her naked body. His shadow overtook her. As the need to imprint himself on her grew, he made a place for himself between her thighs, resting the weight of his body on hers. He buried his hands in her hair, then leisurely tasted her lips, neck, down her collarbone to her breast. When this was over, he wanted Ivy to remember him with every part of her body. Never to forget his possession or the pleasure he made her feel.

Her hands closed over his ribs, and he felt her growing urgency in the desperation of her grip. His body reveled in her urgency, letting it feed his own. She lifted her hips against him, silently begging him to take her. Every single part of his body, down to his smallest cell, gathered the energy he would need to meet this incredible challenge.

He lifted up onto his knees. To his relief, she immediately unbuckled his dress pants. Slick skin greeted him as he pressed intimately against her. He savored the decadent feel of her naked beneath him, his still-covered legs rubbing against her delicate inner thighs. Bare chest to bare chest.

Paxton's drive, to take what he needed and leave her with even more, kicked into full gear. He pressed inside of her. Any logical thinking that remained at this point imploded, leaving him a creature of instinct and emotions. His inner struggle mimicked the rise and fall of their bodies until he pushed them over the edge, into the ultimate oblivion.

But in the quiet aftermath, when the only sound was their labored breathing and her whispered "I love you, Paxton," he found the word still wouldn't come in return. Instead he once again kissed her temple and whispered that everything would be okay. Then he wrapped his body around hers, and prayed he didn't have to make the choice he could see coming.

"I wish to see Paxton, please," Karen McLemore demanded as she approached Ivy's desk.

Without a word Ivy led her through, no longer feeling any need to bother with polite pleasantries. The elder Mrs. McLemore probably wouldn't appreciate them anyway. And Ivy knew, without it being said, that her days here were numbered.

There wasn't any reason to buzz him first. She knew Paxton wasn't in a meeting or on the phone. The last few days he'd spent most of his time staring out the window, trying to make decisions he didn't share with her. Ironic, considering how many times he'd judged her for the same.

She only knew he felt more distant every day, since the moment she'd made the mistake of saying *I love you*. Were the words too much pressure for a man like him? Was it only a matter of time before he decided to leave her? Decided that she wasn't worth fighting his family for?

Ivy wasn't able to ignore professional courtesy, so she opened the door for his grandmother, but didn't glance his way. Karen McLemore strode inside with the confidence of an imperial ruler surveying her domain.

Just as Ivy began to retreat, the imperious command rang out. "Stay!" Then a quieter but no less stern, "This concerns you, too."

That couldn't be good.

Was she about to be fired? Karen McLemore was, after all, the owner of the family corporation. She had the power to do as she wished. And the right to do so.

Even though Ivy had been anticipating this very thing, the thought of trying to find a job right now brought on a wave of nausea. She didn't imagine Paxton's grandmother would skimp on all the details she was sure to pass along to any potential employers who were looking for a reference. That would look good on Ivy's track record...not.

Would Ivy have to move away to be able to support herself and her child? Was history about to repeat itself?

As she froze in quiet panic, Paxton rose from be-

hind his desk. "Grandmother," he said, acknowledg-
ing her in an overly-formal tone.

"Paxton, you have not returned my phone calls."

He stayed silent, keeping his gaze trained on the
older woman. His expression was more somber than
Ivy had ever seen.

Ivy wasn't even aware his grandmother had tried
to contact him. Then again they rarely spoke these
days, except for business. Instead they spent every
moment outside the office in bed, as if desperate to
savor the connection while it lasted.

"I can't really imagine what we would have to say
to each other," he said.

"Well, I can."

Karen strode forward, pulling a stuffed file folder
from her leather portfolio. "The final report from our
private detective came in."

Ivy swallowed hard. *Our?* Had Paxton been aware
of this? Involved in this?

He glanced her way, as if he could read her
thoughts. "The company retains an investigator, but
I've never used him to look into your background."

"You should have," his grandmother said. "They
found something you need to know."

"That Ivy's family was involved in sinking our
ship generations ago?"

That took his grandmother by surprise, something
Ivy imagined didn't happen often. Karen stiffened.
"You knew?"

"Of course." He shared a glance with Ivy. "We
don't have any secrets from one another."

Anymore...*except how you really feel about me.*

His grandmother slammed the file down onto his desk. "Paxton, how could you consort with the enemy? We did not raise you to be led astray by good looks and a willing body."

His face hardened. "Ivy hadn't even been born when that ship went down."

Karen glanced her way. "There's murder in her blood."

"Really? The same way our family tried to kill an innocent woman and her child in retaliation?"

Karen's eyes narrowed. Ivy felt a moment of fear, even though the gaze wasn't directed at her.

But Paxton refused to back down. "We wanted revenge so badly, we would kill a child over something we had no proof of? You don't usually include that part of the story, do you, Grams?"

Karen raised her chin. "We did what was necessary."

"What was necessary was to find the real villain instead of victimizing the innocent."

She was already shaking her head in denial. "We did nothing of the sort."

"Really? I've seen the police reports. There was no evidence against her family."

Shock rippled through Ivy. Tate had spoken about police reports, but Ivy had never seen them. She'd imagined they'd been lost to time.

"And I've seen proof that another party might be responsible." Paxton crossed his arms over his chest.

"Her family is innocent. But I guess your PI didn't dig quite as deep as mine."

As if sensing she was losing her grip on this situation, Karen changed her tactics.

"Paxton, we've always been close." She studied him intently. Ivy would have been squirming by now, but Paxton stood solid. "Your outright rebellion is cause for great concern."

"Maybe I'm starting to see what my family is really like. And it's not something I want to be a part of."

"That can be arranged."

Ivy gasped as the words hit her square in the chest.

Paxton leaned forward, bracing himself against his desk. "Are you threatening me?"

"No, I'm assuring you that I will terminate your employment here if you do not end this relationship immediately."

No. No. Ivy had known this might get rocky, but this—to take Paxton from what he loved, what he was so good at...

"I don't need our family background or name to be successful in business."

"You might. When word gets out that you were sticking it to your secretary."

Ivy gasped at the crude language, but the battle of wills continued without her.

"I've told you before, Grandmother. I will not separate Ivy from her child."

The words were a promise, one Paxton had given her many times, but still he offered no words of love.

"Nor will I condemn her for something neither she nor her family did. They've suffered enough."

He crossed his arms over his chest as if to say, *I can withstand anything you want to throw at me...*

"Clean out your desk."

Pain crossed his face, but his expression quickly smoothed out, hiding any further clues. Then he said, "Done."

"No."

Both of them looked her way. "Paxton, I know this isn't what you want."

His grandmother smirked. "Neither does she. I'm eliminating her meal ticket."

"How can you be so cold?" Ivy demanded, the woman's words crashing like a shock wave over her system. "He's your grandson."

"He needs to be taught a lesson. As do you—we don't need your kind in our family."

Ivy almost caved, but she couldn't. Not after seeing that flash of pain on Paxton's face. Besides, there was nothing to lose now.

"I'm not doing any of this for money. I love Paxton. The last thing I would want would be to separate him from the family that means so much to him."

"Too late."

She looked at Paxton—a man too proud to give in, but with each of his grandmother's words, his hurt pushed to the surface of his cracking facade. This wasn't what she wanted.

"I will not do this to you, Paxton," she said, surprised to see a touch of panic widen his amber eyes.

"The last thing I want is to tear you away from the family you love. And we both know that's where this is headed. It has been for a week now."

That's why he'd been so quiet. And she understood. She truly did.

"Goodbye, Paxton."

Nothing could've hurt more than saying those words. Even the fact that he didn't make a move to stop her.

Sixteen

Ivy put the finishing touches on the table containing the items Tate had donated to the auction at Keller House. Then she stood back and looked over her handiwork.

Not too bad, considering her heart wasn't really in it.

"Thank heaven for a busy week," Willow said as she, too, surveyed the display for tonight's auction. "It's the best thing to take your mind off a man."

Ivy wished it were that easy, but the reminders of Paxton seemed to be everywhere. From trying to find her hair clip in the few boxes she'd hastily packed while Paxton was at work one day—at least one of them still had a job—to her difficulty finding a dress for tonight that would accommodate her thickening waistline.

She couldn't get away from him as easily as he seemed to ignore her.

"Is Tate driving you crazy?"

Willow rolled her eyes. "He's near the end of a book. Nothing like it to make an author grumpy, hungry and reclusive. Kind of like a bear, from what I've heard."

Better to talk about her sister's man problems than her own. Ivy made a noncommittal noise to keep Willow talking.

"It was all I could do to drag him off the island for tonight's auction."

Ivy could fully understand. Before Willow, Tate hadn't had any kind of social life. His only trips off his island had been meetings with his editor. Now he came to family dinners and the occasional event. Not to mention rescuing future sisters-in-law when they needed it.

"Have you heard anything from Paxton?"

Ah, the one question Ivy did not want to face. But there wasn't any point hiding her humiliation from her sisters.

"No," she sighed, stepping back to survey her handiwork. "I would have thought I would at least hear from the lawyer by now. You know, some attempt at future custody arrangements, but…nothing."

The silence was driving her crazy.

"You feeling okay?" she asked as Willow pressed a hand against the base of her spine. "How's your back holding up?"

Ivy was under strict orders to not let Willow lift

anything, though bending over the displays couldn't feel great, either. Her tummy was worthy of her maternity clothes, whereas Ivy was at the barely-bump stage. Her regular clothes were too tight, but maternity clothes hung like a sack.

Then again she wasn't carrying twins like her sister was.

"Doing good," Willow said. "Can't say I'm looking forward to more restrictions coming my way." She turned to Ivy and grinned. "Aren't you glad you didn't get the double blessing?"

Most definitely. But she was finally starting to connect with her pregnancy now that she felt better. Despite the struggles over Paxton, her energy was returning and she felt more physically capable each day. Rubbing lotion on the small mound of her belly, wondering when the child's first movement would happen, took her mind off her aching wish for Paxton.

Suddenly Willow gave a strange squeak that drew Ivy's attention. She glanced up to see Willow's gaze glued on the distance beyond Ivy's shoulder.

"What? Did the doors open early?" Ivy should've had another twenty minutes or so for a quick walk-through with Jasmine.

But when Willow didn't respond, Ivy turned to look for herself. Standing ten feet away was Paxton. Tuxedoed, freshly shaven, way-too-sexy Paxton.

Definitely squeak-worthy.

Willow mumbled, "I'll go let Jasmine know," and turned to leave, but Ivy stopped her.

"No, she's got enough to deal with. I'll handle this."

It was obvious he planned to speak with her by the way he patiently waited, gaze never leaving her. But why would he choose this public venue to confront her again?

Every step of his approach had her breathing harder and faster. Boy, had she missed him, even with all the uncertainty. Her heart wanted him just as much as it had that one magical night so long ago.

"What are you doing here?" she asked, unable to look away from his amber eyes.

He paused a few feet from her, but the way he shifted on his feet told her he wasn't as confident as he looked.

"I wanted to see you. And I thought this might be a good, neutral space." He used that charming grin to full effect. "Besides, I already had a ticket."

"You only now wanted to see me?"

"I had a few things to work out before I could."

She wasn't sure whether to push or ask or wait. It seemed like her every move through all of this had been the wrong one.

So she let him make the next move.

He did. One step closer, then another.

People started to mill about. The doors must have opened finally. "I'm sorry. I have a job today," she said. She needed to focus, not be distracted by Paxton's good looks and the mix of emotions clouding her judgment.

"Wait. Just a few minutes, okay?"

Ivy crossed her arms over her chest, wrinkling her gown, but didn't leave.

"You haven't come to get your stuff," he said. "At least not all of it."

"I've been a little busy." She waved a hand about the room. "Besides, you could always have it packed up and sent to me."

"What if I don't want to?"

His tone wasn't aggravated or even disdainful, but she didn't understand where he was going with this.

In her frustration she threw out, "Donate it."

The last thing she could imagine doing right now was going over there to pack. She simply couldn't.

The past few months had taken too much from her.

Again he moved closer, this time crowding into her personal space. She held her breath, not wanting to smell the unique spicy sent of him, but her lungs overrode her resolve.

So good. So warm.

She glanced up to see his gaze turned on her, as if he could see through her disdainful facade to the aching need underneath. "What if I'd rather you come home?" he murmured. "Where you belong."

"I don't belong there." Not without his love.

"I believe you do." He ran a finger over her cheek. A touch she desperately wished she could have every day for the next fifty years. "You must. Nothing is the same. The bed feels empty. The kitchen is too quiet. The—"

He swallowed hard, his gaze darkening. "I need you. I didn't realize just how much."

"What about your family?" She wanted this so badly, but... "I can't live like that, Paxton, under constant attack, and I won't allow my child to be exposed to that, either."

"I was wrong, Ivy."

Her eyes widened. That was definitely not what she'd expected to hear. "What?"

"I let my loyalty to my family color everything between us. And the truth is, they don't deserve the consideration."

At the risk of sounding like a broken record... "What?" This was so unexpected, she was having trouble taking it in.

"I knew it. But I didn't want to admit it. I had to work through that—you know."

"I understand." She'd spent too much time trying to work through her issues with Paxton before fate took a hand.

"I promise I will never let them hurt you again." He tilted his chin up. "I haven't gotten it all figured out, but I promise to protect you."

"But I know you love them, Paxton. I can't tear you away from that."

"You don't have to. I resigned my position the day you left."

"What? Why haven't I heard about this?"

"They're too busy trying to get me to return to make an announcement. I guess Grandmother didn't think of the things she would put into action with her little ultimatum."

Ivy found herself clutching the lapels of his tuxedo, her attention caught. "How will you live?"

Then realizing what she'd said, she covered her

face. "I'm sorry. That's just what your grandmother would expect me to ask."

He gently uncovered her face. "And just what I do expect, not because you're mercenary, but because you're worried about me."

"You love your work."

"And I can do it somewhere else. Between my savings and investments, I'll be fine. If not, I'll sell my stock in the company. But I'll be fine until I figure out where I'm going. Maybe even start my own company—who knows?"

Ivy marveled at the excitement on his face before he sobered.

"It's for the best, Ivy. It really is. Regardless of whether you come back to me, I think this separation is important. Grandmother needs to understand that I won't be controlled."

He brushed Ivy's lips with his. "And I don't want the world's best assistant afraid to work for me."

She had so many questions, but as the crowd thickened around them, she knew this was not the time. Instead she let herself be swept away by his kiss until she heard her sister Jasmine close by. "Does this mean what I think it means?"

Ivy pulled back with an embarrassed giggle, but Paxton would not let her go far. He kept an arm fully around her.

"I certainly hope so," he said with a satisfied smile.

"I'm so sorry, Jasmine," Ivy said. "I got distracted—"

"I noticed." But Jasmine and Willow were both smiling.

She saw Tate and Royce talking, over near the display table. "We did finish—"

"And it looks gorgeous," Jasmine said as they all moved closer to the display. "Tate is very pleased with what you've done with his donations."

Paxton halted abruptly, jerking Ivy to a stop. "This is from Tate?" he asked, the odd note in his voice causing Ivy to look up to him.

His startled expression quickly morphed into one of intense focus. He leaned forward.

"Yes, some memorabilia we found in the attic," Tate said. "I figured the local history buffs might bid on some of it."

Paxton seemed to study a watch in the middle of the table. He blinked, stepping closer. His face paled. "Tate—"

Then Paxton's grandmother's voice cut through the crowd. "Paxton, I figured I would find you here."

Paxton couldn't have been more shocked than when he surveyed the group that had approached. His entire family was here. That was a pretty important feat, even for his grandmother. He knew for a fact Sierra would have warned him if she'd had advanced notice, but then again he hadn't told any of them he would be attending.

He hadn't spoken to his family since breaking the news of his resignation during a brief appearance at Sunday dinner. He'd crashed it since he hadn't gotten an invitation. Not that he'd have been able to bring himself to eat. The memories had been too bitter.

Grandmother eyed his arm as he automatically pulled Ivy close. "Consorting with the enemy again, I see."

Tate and Royce also stepped close to their women, but it was Royce who spoke. "I'm going to have to ask you to remain civil, Mrs. McLemore, or you'll be asked to leave."

She drew herself even taller than her normally impressive height. "I'll have you know we bought tickets."

"Keller House is mine," Royce said. "This is my event. What I say goes."

Karen McLemore looked back at Ivy. "You have managed to gain some powerful friends."

"No, ma'am," Ivy said, her voice tight but respectful. "This is my family. Family sticks together."

Paxton felt a glow of pride engulf him. A slightly taken-aback look flashed on his grandmother's face before she recovered. "Only if that family survives. It's my job to see that we do."

"But for you it's only survival if you beat out everyone else on the block. When all is said and done, you end up alone."

The rest of Ivy's family murmured their agreement.

"Nevertheless—"

"Grandmother," Paxton interrupted, the truth of what he needed to do finally hitting him square in the chest. "There's something I think you should see…"

"Not now, Paxton."

"Yes now, Grandmother."

The Harden women parted as he led his grandmother to the display Ivy had been finishing when he arrived. He waited silently while she inspected the items on the table donated by Tate Kingston. Anticipation caused his heart to speed up.

He knew the minute she spotted it.

Her breath grew shaky. Out of the corner of his eye, he saw her hand reach out and grasp the man's pocket watch.

The watch with part of his family's insignia engraved on it.

That's when things started to fall apart. With a moan, his grandmother clutched the piece to her heart, and stumbled forward against the display, shaking the table and its contents. Paxton grabbed her, his heartbeat increasing to triple time. He hoped to steady her, but her weakness as she leaned into him alarmed him even more. The swarm of his family around them and the cacophony of voices added to the confusion.

"Grandmother," he said sharply, "can you breathe?"

He heard her draw in a shaky breath, then mutter, "Yes."

He glanced over to see his father on the other side, supporting her. He shot a quick, panicked look at Royce, only to find him already taking control.

"This way, Paxton," he said.

As one large group, they made their way through the staring crowd to a side room.

"I'll be right back. I saw Dr. Michaels in the crowd earlier," Royce said before retreating out the door.

Between them, Paxton and his father settled his grandmother into a chair. She looked awfully pale, with a high flush along her cheekbones. Deep inside Paxton panicked until he felt a hand on his shoulder. Then he saw Ivy reach out another hand to lay it over his grandmother's.

"It will be okay," Ivy said in a soft but firm tone. "The doctor will be here soon. Just breathe, Mrs. McLemore. Slowly in. Slowly out."

His grandmother seemed to lose all care for who Ivy was in that moment and simply held on to her like a lifeline, following her instructions to steady her breath and calm her instinctive panic.

No more than two minutes later, Royce returned with the doctor. Only then did Karen let go of Ivy's hand. They all retreated to give the doctor some space, crowding around the outer edges of the small room with quiet whispers.

Ivy stepped back next to Paxton, laying her hands softly on his arm. He turned and pulled her hard into his embrace, steadying himself with her heat and soft curves.

"I never wanted this," he murmured against her hair.

She lay her hand on his chest, directly over his fast-beating heart. "I know. What happened? Has she had this happen before?"

Paxton shook his head. "I'm not entirely sure."

Dr. Michaels thoroughly checked his grandmother

over, conversing quietly with her and Paxton's father. Slowly her color became less stark, though she was still pale.

Paxton's father caught his eye and motioned him over. Paxton knelt beside the chair, but could sense Ivy standing at his back. Her presence steadied him.

"I think she's okay," Dr. Michael said, "just a bit of a shock to her system, but I would feel better if we ran a few tests at the hospital. Just to make sure there's nothing going on with her heart."

"Yes. Let's go," Paxton said.

"Not yet."

For a woman who was recently so weak, his grandmother's voice was surprisingly stern.

"Mother," his father protested.

"No, son. This must be done first." She patted his hand. "Then we will go."

Paxton braced himself, utterly sure his grandmother was about to go on the attack once more. Those in the room edged closer. Karen pinned Ivy with her gaze, causing Paxton to tense up. She lifted the watch fob. "Where did you find this?"

Confusion clouded Ivy's expression. "It was Tate's."

He stepped forward. "We found it in the attic of Sabatini House. It didn't have any significance to me, so I donated it to the auction."

"It may not be significant to you, young man, but it certainly is to me."

"I'm sorry, Mrs. McLemore," he said. "Does it belong to your family?"

Karen opened the fob, then glanced at Paxton. "You recognized it?"

Paxton nodded. "It's an emblem from the family crest."

"This belonged to my uncle. It disappeared the night he drowned on that ship."

A collective gasp echoed in Paxton's ears. "How?"

"We assumed it was lost with him. The divers never found it or any trace of the body."

Leaving behind a devastated family, including a grieving little girl. "I'm sorry, Grandmother."

"I was his favorite." She glanced up at him, tears watering down her normally strong amber gaze. "He would bring me candy. I would sit on his lap and he would let me play with his pocket watch—this pocket watch—while he talked with the grown-ups." Tears spilled over her well-preserved cheeks. "Then he was gone."

Which explained why she told the story so often.

Tate spoke into the heavy silence. "Ma'am, on behalf of my family, let me extend my sincere apologies. They were the type of people who got what they wanted and didn't care who was hurt in the process."

"So were we..." Karen murmured.

This time she looked at Jasmine, then Willow and finally Ivy. "And you were caught in the cross fire."

Suddenly Karen struggled with her breath, shuddering as she drew it in with visible strain.

"Grandmother, let's get you to the hospital," Paxton insisted.

She nodded, then held the pocket watch out to Tate.

"No, ma'am," he said with the shake of his head. "That doesn't belong to me."

The room quietly cleared as Dr. Michaels called for an ambulance. "They'll meet us at the east entrance," he said when he ended the call. "Easier and more discrete."

As she stood Karen grasped Paxton's arm. "Paxton, darling, please forgive me."

He could, but he wasn't sure he could ever forget.

Then she looked at Ivy, who was standing close behind him. "Young lady, I want you to know, I will welcome you into our family." Suddenly she looked shaken, broken. "I was wrong. I don't know what more to say."

"Nothing," Ivy graciously offered. "Just take care of yourself."

As the group moved to meet the ambulance, Paxton felt an almost painful pull to stay behind with Ivy despite wanting to be with his family. He turned to her, opening his mouth to speak, but nothing came out.

She hugged him close and repeated the same words he'd given to her in comfort. "It's going to be okay, Paxton."

Somehow he knew it would be. Even though he hadn't accomplished all he'd meant to tonight, his purpose was clear.

"I'll be back for you," he said, and he meant it.

Seventeen

"Go ahead home, Ivy," Jasmine said. "It's been a long night. Or would you rather sleep in one of the guest bedrooms upstairs? I don't want you too tired on the road."

"I'll be fine," Ivy mumbled, "but thanks." Then she turned to go. Anything more and the waterworks would start.

She was just tired enough not to be sure she could stop them. Her body hurt more than it usually did after a long night working these events, probably because of her pregnancy. Her legs and feet ached, and she wanted nothing more than to sleep for twelve hours straight.

Unless it was sleeping for twelve hours straight in Paxton's arms.

She checked her phone on the way out—no calls.

Paxton had driven his parents to the hospital, behind the ambulance, with the assurance that he'd call later on, when he knew something more definite. But the hours had passed with nothing but silence. Now Ivy just wanted to curl up in a space of her own and recover from all the ups and downs of today. But she wasn't sure where that space actually was anymore—Paxton's? Auntie's?

She felt like she didn't belong anywhere. And even though Paxton had acted like he loved her, acted like he wanted her, still the words were missing. She needed the assurance of the feelings rather than just her assumption that they were there.

She should be thrilled that her family had been cleared of the accusations from generations ago. That Paxton had come back to her, but the future was no more certain than it had been five hours ago.

Except now her feet hurt.

Pausing beneath the tall lamppost illuminating the front steps of Keller House, Ivy reached up and loosened the pins that secured her updo from her hair so it could fall in waves around her shoulders. Her headache eased slightly. She sighed, wanting to melt into a puddle.

But not yet. Maybe after she got home and had a bath.

But that only made her remember the time that Paxton had washed her hair, and the tears welled once more.

She lingered at the top of the stone steps, in almost the exact same place she had waited for Paxton all those months ago. A long look at the dark navy sky, with its bright stars so clear this far from the city, steadied her.

At least the stars made her smile.

A real smile, not the professional one she'd pasted on her lips for the last few hours.

"Everything will be okay," she said aloud, echoing Paxton's words as she rubbed her baby bump through the soft chiffon of her formal down.

"Ivy."

She glanced down as Paxton's voice reached out to her from the dark, but her movement was too quick. The shadowy landscape around her swirled. She listed to the side, but Paxton caught her before she lost her balance.

"Careful there," he said, pulling her firmly against him. "I can only handle one ambulance ride tonight."

Ivy laughed, just as he'd intended, but let her fingers grasp the lapels of his jacket tighter than normal to steady herself.

"Guess it's been a little longer since I ate than I thought."

"Junior and I can't have that."

What? "Who says it's a boy?"

"Grandmother insists. She couldn't stop telling everyone at the hospital about it."

Out of respect, Ivy only gave a quiet harrumph instead of an insistent one.

"But right now, I'm less worried about him and more worried about you."

"I'll be fine—"

"No." He quietly shut her down. "I know you aren't, Ivy. And that's my fault."

She held her breath a moment longer than normal as he tucked a few loose strands of her hair behind her ear.

"But I'm ready to remedy that."

"What do you mean?" she asked, but wasn't sure she was ready for the answer.

"We've gone about this all wrong, you and I."

Oh yeah. "I'll agree with that."

He buried his other hand in her hair, cupping her head so that she couldn't look away. As if her aching heart would let her do that.

"Well, from here on out, I want to do it right. You deserve that, Ivy."

She shook her head. "I want it to be right for both of us. That's all I care about, Paxton."

He confirmed her words with a kiss, slow and slick, until she couldn't think of anything but the taste and feel of him. Only when she lost all touch with reality did he pull back.

Then to her surprise, he knelt before her on one knee.

"Paxton!"

"Ivy!" He grinned—oh, that smile got her every time—then he reached into his pocket and pulled out a small jeweler's box. Her body went really still.

He popped it open so the light on top of the lamp-post nearby glinted off a central princess-cut diamond. But Ivy barely glanced at it before looking back up into his strong, handsome face.

"Will you marry me, Ivy?" he asked. No bravado, no overconfidence, just a quiet question. "I need you."

As much as she hated to say it, she forced the words out. "I'm sorry, Paxton."

He cocked his head to the side, an unspoken question.

"I can't. Even though you're saying all the right things, it's not the things that I need to know."

Somehow she knew, if he never said the words, she'd spend her whole life wondering if he was willing to risk his heart for her. And he needed to know it, too. Know that he could put the past behind him and move forward with her.

Pulling her hand to his mouth, he pressed a kiss to her skin, then looked up and said, "I love you, Ivy. I love everything about you—you're strong, you're sexy and you stand your ground with my family, without losing your signature grace and poise. I know it. They do, too."

Then he stood. "I hope it's never an issue again, but if it is, know that I'm by your side, no matter what."

There was no mistaking his sincerity as they stood in the moonlight, having come full circle from where this adventure had all started.

There under the stars, he pulled the ring from the jeweler's box, then slipped the box back into his pocket before lifting her hand. The gold band felt cool against her skin as he slipped the ring on to her finger.

"You're stuck with me, Ivy, no matter what the world decides to throw at us."

She smiled at him, knowing that he deserved just

as much from her. Not just her love, but... "And I promise, no more secrets."

He kissed the ring where it encircled her finger. "Except for one," he said.

She glanced up at him.

"The gender reveal. I think we need to keep that secret to ourselves."

Oh, he was naughty. "Your grandmother is going to have a fit."

"Well, we've got to have fun where we can."

Epilogue

The Harden sisters stepped into the hallway at Keller House—Ivy and Jasmine on the outside, with Willow in the middle. All of them were dressed in their own versions of wedding white. Just down the hall, Auntie stood with Rosie and two of Paxton's nieces, each with a basket of flower petals.

Ivy nodded, and the wedding director got everyone underway.

"Whose idea was it to walk half the house to get to the wedding ceremony?" Willow asked with a lighthearted grumble. "I have to pee again."

"You just went," Jasmine exclaimed.

"Doesn't matter when you have two munchkins bouncing on your bladder."

Ivy sympathized. At thirty-eight weeks herself,

she felt like there was definitely no more room at the inn. They'd wanted the wedding before all the babies were born, and this was the only time they'd been able to coordinate for everyone, but they were definitely pushing it a little.

They were lucky Willow had been blessed with an extremely easy pregnancy, despite the twins, and had only had to deal with a few limitations. Bed rest not being one of them.

"Just do your best," Ivy said. "It will be over and party time soon."

"And all you'll remember of your wedding is the urgent need for the bathroom," Jasmine teased.

Which was funny because it was true. So, that's how the Harden sisters arrived at the ballroom door for their wedding, giggling.

They walked into the crowded room as if they were royalty. A very limited amount of exclusive invitations had been given to attend the wedding of the year. Three of Savannah's most notorious bachelors were being wed after making a splash on the social scene with their brides-to-be.

The large room was understated elegance incarnate. The gilded panels and floor-to-ceiling mirrors along one wall were incredibly elegant. Jasmine had chosen antique-white chairs, with gold leafing to compliment the surroundings.

Enormous flower arrangements and tulle bows splashed a mixture of the women's colors in pastel versions of green, blue and rose on the gilded backdrop. The aisle to the altar had been set wide enough to accommodate the three of them as they made their way to the men waiting for them in dark gray suits.

They paused at the end of the aisle, allowing the photographer to take a couple of shots.

Willow sighed, then looked at each of her sisters in turn. "I'd say that ring did an incredible job, right, ladies?"

They shared a smile. Willow had been right all along. The ring had been magical…and it had unleashed a magic in their lives unlike anything they could have imagined. Even in all the fantasies that had gotten Ivy through her lonely teenage years.

"Mother knew just what she was doing when she passed that on to us," Ivy agreed.

Her heart swelled over Paxton's loving gaze as he watched her approach. To marry him with her family celebrating with them and his child nestled deep beneath her ribs was the most enchanted moment she could ever have imagined.

And she didn't miss her glimpse of his family in the front two rows, either. His grandmother had not been happy for her only grandson to share his spotlight on this special day, but she was definitely learning his boundaries…protective barriers he fiercely upheld against everyone, including his family.

Paxton wouldn't be held back, but lowered his head to brush his lips over Ivy's as soon as she arrived, drawing a ripple of comments from the crowd. He grinned, causing her heart to speed up and her body to ask for more.

"We're pretty good at making a splash, huh?" he asked.

"Oh yeah," she said, then glanced at her sisters, only to see the other couples watching them.

"We're ready when you are," Willow said. The crowd laughed.

"You look beautiful, princess," Paxton murmured.

With Paxton, she definitely felt like a princess. Every day he pampered her and cared for her, showing her exactly how much he wanted her and their baby. She was due in just a few short weeks, and they were so excited about the birth of their son.

Not that they had mentioned the gender to anyone…including his grandmother. A fact that always made Paxton laugh.

As the officiant spoke a blessing over the couples, Ivy marveled at how far they'd come as a family. She looked past Paxton to her sisters and their soon-to-be husbands.

Each one unique. Bringing their own history, pain and strengths to their relationships. This year had changed the course of their family. Today they celebrated marriage, but it was also a celebration of family. Triumph. New life.

Then the pastor gave each husband-to-be the chance to speak as they placed the rings on their new wives' fingers.

Royce went first. "Jasmine, until I met you, my life was made up of numbers and spreadsheets. Now it's filled with color and laughter and joy. I promise to put you and our family above all else."

Then Tate. "Willow, you've shown me that life is truly worth living. Not in fear, but in full. I promise never to retreat from the world, or you, again. And to look up from my typewriter every once in a while..."

And Paxton. "Ivy, you are the strongest, most gracious woman I've ever known. You've taught me about trust and love and true connection. As the saying goes, I promise to never leave you nor forsake you. I love you."

As he slid the ring on to her finger to nestle against her engagement ring, Ivy felt a rush of tears that she rapidly blinked away. She met Paxton's gaze and mouthed, "I love you, too."

"I now pronounce you *husbands* and *wives*," the pastor said, his emphasis drawing a laugh from their guests. But Ivy paid no mind as she leaned in for Paxton's firm kiss, eager to seal all the promises they'd made to each other.

The standing ovation from the wedding guests finally pulled them apart. As Ivy stared into the amber eyes that mirrored her own happiness, she heard Willow say, "Well, I almost made it through the whole thing."

Suddenly all eyes were on her very pregnant sister. Jasmine and Ivy both rushed to Willow's side.

"Are you okay?" Ivy asked.

Ever the pragmatist, Willow grimaced. "I really did try to wait, but I think my water just broke."

Her sisters laughed. Jasmine joked, "I don't think that's something you can control."

"I haven't been able to control anything about this pregnancy."

Paxton looked from Willow to Ivy and back. "Honestly, the odds were against a labor-free wedding."

Ivy reached out to Tate, who had gone pale and shaky. "Are you okay?"

"Is this bad?" he asked. "Isn't it awfully early?"

Willow shook her head. "You know the doctor said this might happen. Everything will be fine. But we might want to go on to the hospital, instead of partying. You know, do the responsible-parenting thing."

"Yes, definitely," Tate said.

Royce turned to the crowd. "Ladies and gentlemen, please head into the reception room down the hall. Some of us will join you for the cutting of the cake, but I'm sure you can understand our sense of urgency."

The crowd obediently headed to the back of the room and out the ballroom doors to the dining hall, where the reception had been set up, but the swell of speculation echoed off the mirrored walls. Auntie followed the final trickle of people, holding Rosie by the hand.

"Willow did this just for me," Tate said. "Didn't you, wife?"

"I don't understand," Paxton said.

Willow gave a half grin that turned into a grimace as she bent forward to breathe.

"Contractions already?" Ivy asked, feeling her own face contort into a sympathy-induced frown.

Willow nodded. After a moment she straightened and said, "Tate didn't want to be stuck having to talk to hundreds of people at the reception…"

"Convenient," Paxton said.

Jasmine's event-planner persona kicked in. "Okay, hospital time. We will meet you after we've posed for some pictures with the cakes."

Thank goodness they'd taken all the other wedding photos earlier.

Paxton and Ivy followed the other couples out through the kitchen, where a driver was waiting to take them to the hospital. They watched as the car, with its cute Just Married banner on the back window, gained speed as it headed down the drive.

"Pretty soon it will be our turn," Paxton said.

"I know your grandmother can't wait."

"I can't wait." Paxton placed a quick kiss on Ivy's neck, sending shivers down her spine. "I'm ready for the adventure to begin."

Ivy smiled into Paxton's gorgeous amber eyes, wondering if their baby would be lucky enough to inherit them. "I think it already has."

* * * * *

Don't miss a single
Savannah Sisters novel
by Dani Wade!

A Family for the Billionaire
Taming the Billionaire
Son of Scandal

Available now from Harlequin Desire!

#2653 NEED ME, COWBOY

Copper Ridge • by Maisey Yates

Unfairly labeled by his family's dark reputation, brooding rancher Levi Tucker is done playing by the rules. He demands a new mansion designed by famous architect Faith Grayson, an innocent beauty he would only corrupt...but he *must* have her.

#2654 WILD RIDE RANCHER

Texas Cattleman's Club: Houston • by Maureen Child

Rancher Liam Morrow doesn't trust rich beauty Chloe Hemsworth *or* want to deal with her new business. But when they're trapped by a flash flood, heated debates turn into a wild affair. For the next two weeks, can she prove him wrong without falling for him?

#2655 TEMPORARY TO TEMPTED

The Bachelor Pact • by Jessica Lemmon

Andrea *really* regrets bribing a hot stranger to be her fake wedding date... especially because he's her new boss! But Gage offers a deal: he'll do it in exchange for her not quitting. As long as love isn't involved, he's game...except he can't resist her!

#2656 HIS FOR ONE NIGHT

First Family of Rodeo • by Sarah M. Anderson

When a surprise reunion leads to a one-night stand with Nashville sweetheart Brooke, Flash wants to turn one night into more... But when the rodeo star learns she's been hiding his child, can he trust her, especially when he's made big mistakes of his own?

#2657 ENGAGING THE ENEMY

The Bourbon Brothers • by Reese Ryan

Sexy Parker Abbott wants *more* of her family's land? Kayleigh Jemison refuses—unless he pays double *and* plays her fake boyfriend to trick her ex. Money is no problem, but can he afford desiring the beautiful woman who hates everything his family represents?

#2658 VENGEFUL VOWS

Marriage at First Sight • by Yvonne Lindsay

Peyton wants revenge on Galen's family. And she'll get it through an arranged marriage between them. But Galen is not what she expected, and soon she's sharing his bed and his life...until secrets come to light that will change everything!

Get 4 FREE REWARDS!

We'll send you 2 FREE Books plus 2 FREE Mystery Gifts.

Harlequin® Desire books feature heroes who have it all: wealth, status, incredible good looks... everything but the right woman.

FREE
Value Over
$20

YES! Please send me 2 FREE Harlequin® Desire novels and my 2 FREE gifts (gifts are worth about $10 retail). After receiving them, if I don't wish to receive any more books, I can return the shipping statement marked "cancel." If I don't cancel, I will receive 6 brand-new novels every month and be billed just $4.55 per book in the U.S. or $5.24 per book in Canada. That's a savings of at least 13% off the cover price! It's quite a bargain! Shipping and handling is just 50¢ per book in the U.S. and 75¢ per book in Canada.* I understand that accepting the 2 free books and gifts places me under no obligation to buy anything. I can always return a shipment and cancel at any time. The free books and gifts are mine to keep no matter what I decide.

225/326 HDN GMYU

Name (please print)

Address   Apt. #

City   State/Province   Zip/Postal Code

Mail to the **Reader Service:**
IN U.S.A.: P.O. Box 1341, Buffalo, NY 14240-8531
IN CANADA: P.O. Box 603, Fort Erie, Ontario L2A 5X3

Want to try 2 free books from another series? Call 1-800-873-8635 or visit www.ReaderService.com.

---

*Terms and prices subject to change without notice. Prices do not include sales taxes, which will be charged (if applicable) based on your state or country of residence. Canadian residents will be charged applicable taxes. Offer not valid in Quebec. This offer is limited to one order per household. Books received may not be as shown. Not valid for current subscribers to Harlequin Desire books. All orders subject to approval. Credit or debit balances in a customer's account(s) may be offset by any other outstanding balance owed by or to the customer. Please allow 4 to 6 weeks for delivery. Offer available while quantities last.

Your Privacy—The Reader Service is committed to protecting your privacy. Our Privacy Policy is available online at www.ReaderService.com or upon request from the Reader Service. We make a portion of our mailing list available to reputable third parties that offer products we believe may interest you. If you prefer that we not exchange your name with third parties, or if you wish to clarify or modify your communication preferences, please visit us at www.ReaderService.com/consumerschoice or write to us at Reader Service Preference Service, P.O. Box 9062, Buffalo, NY 14240-9062. Include your complete name and address.

HD19R

*Unfairly labeled by his family's dark reputation,
brooding rancher Levi Tucker is done playing by the
rules. He demands a new mansion designed by famous
architect Faith Grayson, an innocent beauty he would
only corrupt…but he* must *have her.*

Read on for a sneak peek at
Need Me, Cowboy
by New York Times *bestselling author Maisey Yates!*

Faith had designed buildings that had changed skylines,
and she'd done homes for the rich and the famous.

Levi Tucker was something else. He was infamous.

The self-made millionaire who had spent the past five
years in prison and was now digging his way back…

He wanted her. And yeah, it interested her.

She let out a long, slow breath as she rounded the
final curve on the mountain driveway, the vacant lot
coming into view. But it wasn't the lot, or the scenery
surrounding it, that stood out in her vision first and
foremost. No, it was the man, with his hands shoved
into the pockets of his battered jeans, worn cowboy
boots on his feet. He had on a black T-shirt, in spite of
the morning chill, and a black cowboy hat was pressed
firmly on his head.

She had researched him, obviously. She knew what he looked like, but she supposed she hadn't had a sense of…the scale of him.

Strange, because she was usually pretty good at picking up on those kinds of things in photographs.

And yet, she had not been able to accurately form a picture of the man in her mind. And when she got out of the car, she was struck by the way he seemed to fill this vast, empty space.

That also didn't make any sense.

He was big. Over six feet and with broad shoulders, but he didn't fill this space. Not literally.

But she could feel his presence as soon as the cold air wrapped itself around her body upon exiting the car.

And when his ice-blue eyes connected with hers, she drew in a breath. She was certain he filled her lungs, too.

Because that air no longer felt cold. It felt hot. Impossibly so.

Because those blue eyes burned with something.

Rage. Anger.

Not at her—in fact, his expression seemed almost friendly.

But there was something simmering beneath the surface…and it had touched her already.

Don't miss what happens next!
Need Me, Cowboy
by New York Times *bestselling author Maisey Yates.*

Available April 2019 wherever
Harlequin® Desire books and ebooks are sold.

www.Harlequin.com

Want to give in to temptation with
steamy tales of irresistible desire?

Check out **Harlequin® Presents®,
Harlequin® Desire** and
Harlequin® Kimani™ Romance books!

New books available every month!

CONNECT WITH US AT:

Facebook.com/groups/HarlequinConnection

Facebook.com/HarlequinBooks

Twitter.com/HarlequinBooks

Instagram.com/HarlequinBooks

Pinterest.com/HarlequinBooks

ReaderService.com

**ROMANCE WHEN
YOU NEED IT**

PGENRE2018

Love Harlequin romance?

DISCOVER.

Be the first to find out about promotions, news and exclusive content!

f Facebook.com/HarlequinBooks

Twitter.com/HarlequinBooks

Instagram.com/HarlequinBooks

Pinterest.com/HarlequinBooks

ReaderService.com

EXPLORE.

Sign up for the Harlequin e-newsletter and download a free book from any series at **TryHarlequin.com.**

CONNECT.

Join our Harlequin community to share your thoughts and connect with other romance readers!
Facebook.com/groups/HarlequinConnection

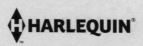

**ROMANCE WHEN
YOU NEED IT**

THE WORLD IS BETTER WITH

Romance

Harlequin has everything from contemporary, passionate and heartwarming to suspenseful and inspirational stories.

Whatever your mood, we have a romance just for you!

Connect with us to find your next great read, special offers and more.